PG.EDG-155

D0123746

THE
SEVENTH PRAYER

Nancy Talley

iUniverse, Inc.
Bloomington

THE SEVENTH PRAYER

This is a work of fiction. All of the characters, names, incidents,
organizations, and dialogue in this novel are either the products
of the author's imagination or are used fictitiously.

iUniverse books may be ordered through booksellers or by contacting:

iUniverse
1663 Liberty Drive
Bloomington, IN 47403
www.iuniverse.com
1-800-Authors (1-800-288-4677)

ISBN: 978-1-4502-6524-9 (pbk)
ISBN: 978-1-4502-6525-6 (ebk)

Printed in the United States of America

iUniverse rev. date: 12/16/2010

THE

SEVENTH PRAYER

Michael:
"War isn't a tear in the fabric of things, it is the fabric.
If the earth is our mother, our father is war."
Lee Blessing CE
TWO ROOMS: Act 1, Scene 2. Page 20.

"And no grown up will ever understand
that this is a matter of so much importance."
Antoine de Saint-Exupery CE
THE LITTLE PRINCE

Chapter 1
SIMON

"The problem is simple: we cannot enforce wisdom.
Each generation must gain it for themselves."

Maria Nu of the Americas LW700
THIRD RIGHTS OF THE PEOPLE
CONFERENCE: WHITE PAPER

The morning was still fairly cool. A breeze off the river, sharp and clean, left the air breathable. Later the humidity would make his lungs feel heavy, his body sluggish. The trees outside Simon's bedroom windows looked particularly green, that bright light green which only shows itself in certain lights in early spring. The soft scent of narcissus and early marsh grass spread through his room. Simon stretched, feeling the smooth sheets against the tops of his feet.

He reached for one of his journals stacked on the nightstand, opened the lined pages to a place where the pages fell naturally. The night before he had begun reading his old journals and three of them still sat on the small wooden table next to his bed. This morning he read: "Tuesday: Today I told my sister she was mean. She made fun of me when I got home from my first day at the Training Center. Wednesday: Today I saw Cristin. I think I love her. Thursday: Today Father invited me to come to his woodshop. I swept up the shavings. The wood smelled good. Friday: This morning when I woke up I had an erection. It was nice but I felt embarrassed. I don't like having to write in this book every day. There are some things I just don't want to write down even if no one ever reads it but me."

Simon remembered when he was twelve, when he had begun the journals. At the time it didn't seem important, but now, almost six years later, he could see how reading it over could help him remember himself, get to know himself. He took his pen in hand and wrote, "This is the last time I will have to write in my journal. Today is the first day of my Beginning. I am afraid. Why didn't anyone tell me more about the Pilgrimage?"

He put the pen in the drawer of the nightstand, laid the journal on top of the others stacked on the lower shelf of this table his father had crafted by hand, in his workshop behind the house. Simon rolled over and sat up on the edge of the bed. "It is a good day to begin a Pilgrimage." He spoke aloud to himself, trying to reassure himself against his fears. He smiled, wiggled his toes, and felt the smooth paneled floor under his bare feet. The floor felt solid. The floor felt good.

He was glad he had decided to make his Pilgrimage before his years of Service to the Corps, even though most of his friends planned to wait. Simon wanted to go on his Pilgrimage now, before he entered his career, before he married. He thought of his sisters, thought how lucky they were because they made their Pilgrimage at the age of twelve, before the age of decision-making. The girls didn't have to make a choice. "Girls are lucky." He spoke aloud again. Realizing someone might hear, he put his hand to his mouth as a reminder to keep his thoughts quiet. His mother had a way of putting her fingers to her lips when she wanted inner privacy. Why had he never realized that before this morning? He felt like he was waking up inside in a way he had not experienced before.

Simon thought about his preparations, the things he must take with him. Most of his packing was done. What he needed from his personal belongings was minimal. He had already packed his shaver, mouth cleaning kit, his comb and brush, his Card. The rest of what he would carry was in the attic in the heavy wooden trunk stored under the eves of the house.

That trunk had been stored in the attic for as long as Simon could remember. Once a year Simon helped his father bring the trunk down from the attic. It was his father's task, as eldest male in the family, to remove the garments stored there, to see that they were aired and cleaned, make any repairs that might be needed, then to pack them again into their natural fiber wrappings. The trunk was then closed and locked for another year, or until the oldest male child was ready to make his Pilgrimage. Someday this seemingly simple task would be Simon's responsibility; it would be his duty to his family. Simon remembered how each year when the contents of the trunk were removed and cleaned, his father would tell the family the same thing.

He told them, "Caring properly for these garments is a small task compared to the gift they represent." His father always whistled a tuneless little melody on the day he opened the trunk and cleaned the garments. Simon thought it strange that he would remember that little fact now, while he was preparing for one of the most important events of his life.

As the time approached to go downstairs to join his family, Simon felt hesitant, a little shy. He realized he was hungry, ready to break the fast they had held in honor of his Beginning. Yesterday the family had not taken any nourishment other than unleavened bread and water. His stomach rumbled and a vision of fresh melon popped into his head. He shook the picture away with a toss of his head, but hurried to get downstairs.

This morning they would share the breakfast prepared for every young man on the day of that young man's Beginning. Simon thought about his sisters, imagined they would smile and perhaps be a little smug. After all they had made their journey four and five years ago. He hoped they would have some understanding of the journey Simon was about to begin even though on their Pilgrimage he had heard that they had not entered all of the rings of the Holy Structure as Simon would. He wondered if they would be envious.

He pulled on his biosuit wondering why there were no special garments for the women, why only the men of the family would walk the Last Mile wearing the Ancient Clothing so carefully stored and cared for. "I wonder why I never asked them that," he mumbled to himself as he started down the hall toward the bathroom. He realized he was becoming more nervous as the time to face his family came closer. He had never felt nervous about being with them before. Suddenly his head was full of questions and he knew he had no time to ask them.

On this special morning his father would light the fire in the kitchen fireplace. He would burn the sacred logs laid the night before. His mother would cook the traditional porridge over that fire in a kettle made of real iron, which hung from a hook over the flames. Simon knew the family had burned fires of real wood on the occasions of the birth of his sisters. His father had built a wood fire to welcome his daughters into the home. But when that happened, Simon was too young to care about such things. This fire was built to celebrate Simon's Pilgrimage.

Simon's father told him that the sacred wood for this morning's fire came from the tree planted on the day Simon was born. Each father who lived in a rural Colony planted a tree on the day a male child was born. He also planted a tree when a girl was born, but the wood from that tree was only burned if she gave birth to a girl child. Things seemed easier for girls Simon thought. He wondered where the sacred wood came from if a boy lived in the city. Perhaps in the urban sections of the Colony a Priest said holy words over bioboard logs to make them sacred. Perhaps another expression of the sacred fire was allowed on the day of the Beginning. Did they have hearth fires in the city? Simon had meant to ask his father about these things, but he had forgotten.

Simon walked slowly down the broad staircase running his hand along the wooden handrail. He wanted to remember how things felt, how they smelled, what they looked like. This would be his last meal with his family for many days. He had never been away from his family, or from the Colony for more than a day. He had attended his Training classes in the Colony, and helped his family with the chores of running the home. He had taken his Fitness Training and studied the Training Manuals in preparation for his years of Service in the Corps.

He knew he would have to serve two years in the Corps. He looked forward to it. He didn't mind the idea of being away from home for two years, but he wanted to go on his Pilgrimage as soon as it was allowed. He had heard the men in his family speak of the Holy Structure, and from the time he was a little boy he had wondered what it must be like. His father told him the Holy Structure was built by Craftsmen, that their workmanship was done entirely by hand. The Craftsmen used no bioboards, no plastine, nothing synthetic. Simon could hardly wait to see for himself.

As a small boy Simon had watched his father at the Craft of

woodworking, watched him cut, smooth, drill, turn, fit and join, then finish the wood with stains, hot oil and wax. He had watched the forms take on shape, changing from rough lumber to banisters, shelves, chests, chairs, and tables. Their family home even had a kitchen floor made entirely of wood; his father had fashioned a floor of the small left over pieces from his other projects. No one else Simon knew had wooden floors.

His father had told him, as Simon sat among the wood shavings, smelling the sweet aromatic scent, that only a very few men in the Colonies were allowed to work at a Craft. In the Holy Structure, all of the old Crafts were worked and the old skills kept in tact. Simon longed to see what he could not imagine.

The wooden banister under Simon's hand felt warm and resilient. He knew that if his father had not been allowed to keep the Craft of woodworking, this banister would be made of plastine or bioboards like the banisters in the other homes he visited. The real wood felt responsive under his hand. He tried to imagine the Holy Structure where every part was made of natural materials, where even the tools and utensils were made by hand.

Today, on the day of his Beginning, his mother would bring out the old things, the family relics, and he would be allowed to handle them for the first time. The family would use them today and then they would be put away until the next male child had his Beginning. This use would have to be enough.

Simon had seen the wooden box his father had built for his mother's kitchen. He had seen her remove the contents, clean them, wash the tablecloth and put them all away again with loving care. It had not, until today, occurred to him that these homely utensils were of any particular value. Now, thinking about how few things were still made of natural materials, he began to realize why these relics were so cherished and protected.

For the first time Simon thought about the men of his family who had held a real glass, lifted the porridge to their mouths with a wooden spoon, felt the cracked and roughened edge of a ceramic bowl against their lips. Had his grandfathers, his uncles, been as timid and excited as he felt this morning?

Simon was frightened, excited, and happy all at the same time. These traditions begun many, many years ago had been repeated generation after generation, had held their strength and power since a time very soon after the Last War. No one he knew questioned these rites of passage. No one ever asked if a young man might not go on his Pilgrimage. It was simply taken for-granted each young man would go on his Pilgrimage soon after his eighteenth birthday, or soon after he returned from his Service in the Corps.

Simon arrived at the kitchen door as his mother was laying out the clay bowls, the wooden spoons, the glasses molded from real glass. She did not see him standing in the doorway. He looked at this room he had seen so often, now seeing it with new eyes. He saw the table his father had made, saw its round, spooled legs. He looked at the shelves made for the plates they used each day for their meals. Plates made of white plastine, without decoration. Plain cups. Plain bowls. He saw the fireplace blazing, with the cauldron hanging over the fire. His mother must have risen early. Curtainless windows looked out on the vegetable garden. He wondered how urban families got their vegetables and herbs. It seemed strange that he had never thought about these things before. It was a pleasant room, warm and inviting. He wanted to go in but hesitated at

7

the door, watching the women in his family working together. He had a catch in his throat. He did not want to speak for fear they would hear the tears behind his eyes.

Simon's mother laid the relics on the food cloth her grandmother had woven. Simon knew his Great-Grandmother was the only other member of the family who had been allowed to keep a Craft. Only the women were allowed to weave, and only if they wanted to, but very few did. Simon watched his sisters helping his mother with the table, handling the relics as if this was an everyday event. They were allowed to handle the precious clay bowls, the metal spoons bent with age, the cloth napkins, only because they had already made their Pilgrimages.

One day one of his sisters would carry these relics to her home, carry them to her kitchen in the same wooden box her mother used. As he watched the girls help his mother set the table he wondered which one of them would be allowed to marry and carry a child, to become part of a new family. Which one would keep the relics? He was beginning to accept the fact that he would never know what happened to either of his sisters on their Pilgrimages.

Simon thought about the lessons from school. Strange, disconnected thoughts ran through his mind. During his years of Training, Simon and all the other young people in his Colony had learned that the population of Earth had become so over crowded before the Last War that their had been mass starvation, disease and suffering. The Elders no longer allowed people to marry, to have children simply because they wanted to. Marriage and child rearing had to be controlled to avoid poverty, and deprivation, and the rules were becoming increasingly strict as the world population grew.

As he watched from the door, Simon quietly wished that Amy

would be chosen to bear a child, as she had wanted a family from the time she was a little girl. Amy was the one who always wanted to play with the soft rag doll her grandmother had made from scraps of cloth her mother had woven. Lucy wanted to become a Priestess. It did not occur to Simon to question the decision. He was confident it would be a wise one and that the Elders would take the feelings of the girls into consideration. Their aunt worked as a Trainer at the International Conference of Trainers and Clerics. She lived a good life, enjoyed her work, and never seemed to miss having children. Perhaps Lucy would like that kind of life.

"Good morning." He heard himself speak and his voice came as a surprise. He had been lost deep in thought.

"Good morning Simon" said his mother as she came over to give him a hug. "How are you feeling on this very special day?" she asked with a smile.

Her smile comforted him a bit and he relaxed a little. He looked expectantly at Lucy and Amy but they were busy setting the table and stirring the porridge. They seemed not to notice him. "Good morning, Lucy. Good morning, Amy." He spoke with some hesitation not knowing how they would behave toward him.

"Hi!" said Amy. Lucy just smiled.

Everything seemed to be all right. Simon knew it was an honor for Amy and Lucy to be allowed to set out the relics and to arrange them on the food cloth. It was a special day for them too. Everyone seemed to be on best behavior; his worry about being teased began to fade. Lucy adjusted the food cloth Great Grandmother had woven when the previous one was so worn it could not be used. The good parts of the old cloth had been

9

saved for small projects such as dolls, and the worn parts saved for felting, or used to stuff pillows. Someday when this cloth became too worn to use, one of their great grandmother's descendants would learn to weave in order to make another.

As he stood and watched from the kitchen door, seeing the tenderness and care these women gave to their task, Simon wondered if all this preparation might not be too much trouble, too much bother to go through just because a male child was going on a trip.

"I hope you're hungry," said his mother.

"Oh I am," said Simon, not at all sure what else he could possibly say.

His family looked beautiful to him on this spring morning. Perhaps because he was going to be parted from them for the first time in his young life, perhaps because he had never really stepped aside from the everyday chores and activities of their life together to look at them objectively. His sisters had become young women. Simon wondered why he hadn't noticed?

Amy stepped into the hallway. Simon took her arm and whispered, "Amy, can I talk with you for a few minutes?"

Amy glanced at their mother, busy in the kitchen, and said, "I guess so, until Mother calls for me. What do you want?"

Simon took a deep breath and asked, "Do you think I will be any different when I get home from my Pilgrimage, you know, not like I am now?"

Amy smiled and looked right into his eyes. She put one hand on her hip, cocked her head the way she always did, and said,

"You have been practicing being yourself for almost eighteen years. What makes you think a week or so will change you? Go read your journals. That is who you are. You are my big brother and you always will be. Does that answer your question?"

"I guess so." said Simon, but he wasn't sure. "…and I have been reading my journals.", he insisted. Their mother called to Amy and she went back to the kitchen to help with the meal preparations.

Simon's father came in with another armload of wood for the fire. His father was a strong man, physically fit and powerful. He was stronger than most men of his age were because he had kept a Craft, a Craft requiring hard physical work. It was a big expense for the family to carry, what with the tools, the shop, the various woods, but it was worth it because his father was at peace. Simon knew most men never received permission to work at a Craft.

The word "Craft" sounded old and strange as Simon ran it around in his head, but it also sounded warm and worn like the banister had felt under his hand earlier. Simon had never thought to ask his father whether he would be allowed to learn a Craft. It suddenly occurred to him that there were a lot of questions in his mind, questions he had not been concerned with before.

Simon was not ready to enter the room. He liked watching his family, liked watching the girls learn about the relics from their mother. He watched his mother as she instructed the girls in food preparation for this breaking of the fast. Simon couldn't help but wonder why people had done all that work for so long. The new ways, with micro-power, were much faster and more efficient, but somehow they seemed almost to lack something by comparison. The new ways are faster but… Simon lost the thought. Perhaps the olden-day people did have better ways, but watching his family work at this meal he concluded that no one would want to do things the old way now, no one in his right mind.

"Where did they get the wood for the fires in the olden times?" he asked. No one answered. They were all too busy with their tasks. He knew the supply of natural materials left on earth would not be adequate to make the old ways work. It was just too much for his head to even consider this morning, but Simon did think about the satisfaction they must have felt as they worked. He could see, when he was in the woodshop, his father took deep pride in his Craft.

He looked at his sisters, watching the gentleness with which they arranged the relics. One of them, he hoped, would someday teach her daughter these quiet, homey rituals. But, by then, the new edicts would be in force, and she would have only one daughter or one son. He suddenly knew that neither of his sisters might ever do this simple task again unless one of the girls was allowed to marry and gave birth to a girl. It somehow all seemed confusing.

"Anyway, " he thought aloud to himself, "Today is not a day to dwell on such things. Today is a day of thanksgiving."

The family sat at the table just as they always had, but the porridge tasted strange and felt thick in his mouth. Simon found a lump. He said nothing, as he would never want to embarrass his mother. She had prepared the food from recipes in the ancient food box, which had been her great-grandmother's. The papers had long ago disintegrated and been replaced with plastine, but the box was still intact. It had been in his family for ten generations if you believed the stories. He could still see the faint tinge of some color on the metal, perhaps a flower petal and a stem.

Simon had been in friend's homes and he had seen food boxes made of wood, but only a few because they did not last as long as the metal ones. Each of the families he knew had a few relics made of metal among their Pilgrimage relics. He had seen metal forks, metal knives, and once a metal pitcher said to have held milk from the owner's own cow. He could not help but wonder what it must have been like when porridge grains grew in great open fields and families sat down to eat home cooked porridge together every day.

Simon sat with his family and ate the sacred food with the sacred relics. They did not say much. It was hard to know what to say. He could feel the love and joy his family shared with him on this special day. This was the day of the Beginning of his Pilgrimage. He would miss these beloved people on his journey. He struggled to think of something special to say, but found no words. He smiled at Amy across the table.

They finished their breakfast in silence. The girls helped clean up after the meal. Simon and his father waited in the common room. All that was left to do now was the Donning of the Clothes. They would need to wait for the other men in the family to arrive and for an Elder to come to the house. It was only eight o'clock, but it seemed like hours had passed since he had wakened at six.

Every young man knew about the Donning. Simon and his friends had spoken of it many times wondering what it would be like when it finally happened. The Donning was a simple ritual designed to teach the Pilgrim how to wear and care for the garments in the trunk. The trunk had already been carried from the attic. His father must have done that early, soon after starting the Holy Fire. The eldest male in the family would open the trunk.

An Elder would sing the Donning Song while laying the garments out on a long table. Simon's father would instruct him in the Donning so that he would know how to do it for himself when he arrived at the Holy Structure. Simon would walk the Last Mile wearing these garments as his father had done before him. He did not want to disappoint his family in any way.

The words of the Donning Song ran through Simon's head like childhood verse. He supposed that the words had made sense a long time ago, but now they seemed like nonsense. He had heard the word "loom" and the word "warp" from his great-grandmother. He had heard about "war" and "famine" in Training. Obscure references to primitive agriculture and production seemed irrelevant. Simon didn't understand much of the old language. "Tractor." What was a tractor? He had learned the song much as a small child learns a nursery rhyme, memorizing the syllables without grasping the meaning. As the words ran through his head, he wondered if someday one of the modern songwriters would create a more reasonable song, one the young people of today would like to hear, one they would understand.

Simon thought about saying good-bye to his family. They all understood that after he donned the clothes, no woman of the Colony could touch him until he had completed his journey. Simon decided he had better hug his mother and sisters now before he forgot in the excitement. He hesitated. His sisters would probably giggle, but he decided he didn't care.

Simon walked into the kitchen, tapped Amy on the shoulder and gave her a quick hug. She hugged him back. Lucy hugged him and gave him a quick kiss on the cheek. No one giggled. Amy had tears in her eyes and Simon's mother cried openly. Her only son was finally going on his Pilgrimage.

The Elder arrived shortly after eight-thirty followed by Simon's uncles and the rest of the family. Simon's male cousin, two years older, had decided to do his Service to the Corps first, then make his Pilgrimage This meant Simon was the first young male in this generation to go through the Donning. Simon felt shy knowing the girls would watch. The family bathing didn't seem to help at all. It was different when they all took off their clothes and sat in the water together. This time Simon would be the only one to remove clothing. Simon's lovely girl cousin Cristin would be there, watching. He wondered if he would have an erection.

He had heard frightening stories from a friend whose penis stood erect through the entire ritual. Simon prayed for a flaccid penis. The darned thing seemed to have a mind of its own. Even the Priestess he had gone to for pre-pilgrimage counseling had been of no comfort when he spoke of his erection fears. She had simply said it was a common fear and perhaps prayer would help.

Prayer was not a very real event in Simon's young life. From the time he had been a little boy Simon had heard about the Seven Life Prayers. He knew they were important. From time to time he caught himself making a silent request of some unknown power, but he was never very serious about these small wishes. At the weekly Gatherings some families attended, they spoke aloud, and this speaking was sometimes referred to as prayer. Simon's family had elected not to attend Gatherings, so his only knowledge of prayer was from what his friends had told him.

Simon believed however that the Seven Life Prayers he was to pray on his Pilgrimage would really be answered. He worried that he might actually get what he prayed for. He would have to think carefully about the prayers; they seemed a terrible responsibility. He knew he would need to make his Seven Life Prayers at the Holy Structure, and he knew he was not prepared. He would need to think about it on his journey.

Simon had prayed one serious prayer in his life. He had prayed that Cristin would not meet another man while he was away at his Service in the Corps. This was the one prayer Simon was sure of, the one of the Seven Life Prayers he knew he would offer at the Holy Structure. Simon was in love with his cousin Cristin. He had loved her from the time he was fourteen. Last summer she confessed her love for him. They agreed in the warmth of a spring evening that they had an understanding. They decided not to say anything to their parents until Simon returned from his Pilgrimage. In any event, they could not marry without the permission of an Elder, and not until they were both at least twenty-five years old.

Simon's father and the Elder carried the trunk and set it in the common room. The Donning was about to begin. Simon's father turned the old iron key in the lock and opened the trunk. The contents smelled old and dusty compared with modern, odorless ecofibers. Carefully his father removed the garments from the trunk and laid them on the table one by one. They seemed to Simon to belong there with the woven food cloth that had so recently cushioned the other relics.

Each piece of clothing was very old but not worn out. When the time came that one of these wore out, it would be burned in the Holy Fire. That garment would need to be replaced with a new one made in the old ways, so it was much easier to take good care of the old ones. Simon's mother had told him of a family who had had to replace their garments, a family who had not invested against that possibility. They paid dearly for new clothing made in the old ways. A son's Pilgrimage and a marriage had to be delayed for more than a year because of the cost. Simon vowed to himself to take good care of each item of clothing while he walked the Last Mile, while he took part in the ceremony he had imagined so many times.

Simon took off his foot coverings and thermal linings. He removed his biosuit, slipped out of his thermal-shirt, and finally removed his underwear. He stood very still. Surprisingly enough he was not self-conscious. His father read the instructions for the Donning of each of the garments. "The stockings shall be folded down from the top and pulled gently over the foot, starting at the toes, covering the heels…" The family stood by quietly. Simon knew he was not going to have a problem with his penis. The occasion was much too solemn.

The garments consisted of the ancient clothing: underpants and an undershirt, an outer shirt with a collar, a long folded item referred to as a "necktie", stockings with a pattern woven into the cloth, trousers with a metal fastener called a zipper that went up and down an opening in the front, a vest with round disks called buttons, a short coat, and finally shoes made of real leather. One by one, as his father read from the crisp, yellow pages, Simon put on the items of clothing.

The last garment was a long robe, which covered the body from hooded head to the ground. The hem of the robe was frayed from trailing on the ground. The robe had protected men in this family for an unknown number of generations. It was made of a strong cloth called linen. This long robe would protect Simon and the garments from the sunrays of the Unending Desert.

"…and lastly you shall don the robe, pulling the hood over your head to protect yourself from the …." The words blurred in his mind.

Item by item Simon put on the clothes. As he put on each piece, he felt a deep connection with the other men of his family. His father had donned the clothes. His grandfather had donned the clothes. His male cousin would don the clothes in two more years. The sash, which held the robe closed, was so old no one could remember where it had come from. These were the clothes he would wear when he walked the Last Mile, the clothes he would wear when he entered the Holy Structure. Simon was excited, frightened, and keenly aware of himself and the family of people gathered around him.

Learning to fold and pack the garments completed the ritual. He would need to know how to pack the clothes for himself, as he could not wear them on the journey. Only when he arrived at the place where he would begin to walk The Last Mile would he put on these clothes again. Now, ready to leave, he could not touch his mother, his sisters, or his cousin. He wished he had kissed Cristin before the ceremony. He almost spoke to her, but caught himself in time.

He embraced his father first, then the other men in his family. Simon thanked the Elder for attending. She smiled and said nothing.

Chapter 2
THE BEGINNING

"The day will come when all people will be free
to cross borders, when borders will be nothing
but faded lines on antique maps, when the
earth family will finally walk together."

Loni of the Islands LW137
Old Women's Writings.

Simon said goodbye to his family, closed the door to his home, and left. He had everything he needed in his small backpack. The Master Planners had made it easy to travel, and he was grateful for the translator strapped to his wrist. He had never been in any Colony where a language other than American was spoken. He had studied European but was not very good at it. As he walked to the travel center he thought about the ancient methods of exchange, which required something called money. Running his fingers along the tops of the railings, he wondered where people had kept money when they traveled. It seemed to him they would have needed a lot of it.

His studies taught that a traveler in ancient times had to keep track of different kinds of money for different countries. They had to plan their own transportations. It must have been difficult and cumbersome. He felt for the Card in his biosuit pocket and sighed at the thought that the Card made it all so much easier.

The Card, which Simon carried in the chest pocket of his biosuit, kept track of all forms of exchange, all wages, all taxes, all purchases and expenses. The Card made it possible to keep track of the financial life planning of each person who worked, including his mother's work as a keeper of the home. It facilitated financial accountability, wages, and taxes with the office of the Master Planners. He would enter what information he wanted to send, run the Card through the decoder and all the information was sent to the office of the Master Planners. Simon couldn't help but think that primitive times must have been confusing and very difficult.

He slipped his Card through the slot on the decoder and stepped onto the beltway. He watched the other people as the mover took him toward the Travel Center. He wondered if any of the other young men out that morning were beginning their Pilgrimage. There was no way to tell just by looking. The biosuits everyone wore were similar in design, only the colors varied. Even young men going to classes carried a small bag for their books. His Donning clothes fit well into a similar bag. He watched the other young men carefully but could not tell where they were going. He was afraid to ask. He waved to friend from the Training Center, but he was too far away to speak to him.

At the Travel Center Simon went in search of his transport. He found an information kiosk, placed his card in the slot, and waited for instructions. The information bank asked his destination. He typed in "THE HOLY STRUCTURE." He glanced over his shoulder to see if anyone saw his destination, but there was no one else in line. Instructions came indicating he would first need to take mover L to the next transport gate and wait for one hour. He was glad of the delay, as he would have time to eat. The porridge had been satisfying to the soul but had not done much for his body. The local food room would provide a choice of snacks or a meal and a chair until his transport was ready.

It should have been one of the most exciting days of his life. Instead he felt overwhelmed and anxious. Nothing felt right. Simon had never had any occasion to travel this far from home alone. He wished he had brought along one of the history journals, which had explained travel in ancient times. It would have been a good thing to study while he waited. He remembered individual vehicles had actually moved along roads or tracks or through the air. It must have taken incredibly long periods of time. This trip was complicated enough. The travel instructions showed he would have three destinations on three transports before he arrived at his final destination, at the place where he would don the clothes he carried for the final walk.

"Why walk?" he said aloud. Quickly he looked around to see if anyone had heard him. He felt a little silly. Simon wondered to himself about the walk - why was it so important? Some people claimed to walk for pleasure and relaxation, but Simon had not found it satisfactory. He preferred biowork and physio-meditation with weights. Some of the people Simon knew walked to their work every day, but his father worked in his home so Simon had never really thought about it before.

Simon tried to imagine what it must have been like when people had control of individual machines that moved under their own power. He could not imagine entering a machine and making it go where he wanted it to go. It must have been terribly dangerous with so many people going every which way. He shuddered to think of the possible accidents. Life was so much safer now and there was no need to make another decision once you entered the transport.

The hour passed so quickly he almost missed the signal-light for mover L to the East. Simon entered the transport, sat down in a chair, and fastened the belt. He placed his pack in the adjunct container and went to sleep. It was not a particularly restful sleep. He dreamed of a trip where a transporter took him back in time. In his dream there were strange flying machines, flying animals, people walking around on the streets. None of them had ever heard of the Holy Structure or of his Pilgrimage. It was a disturbing dream. He wakened with a start to find himself arriving at the East Gate. He decided that next time he would ask for a sleep-tablet. Unbuckling the belt, releasing his pack, he went in search of the next mover on his list. He had no idea how much time had passed. He decided it didn't matter.

Looking around, he saw that the people of the East had dark skin, dark hair, and dark beautiful eyes. Simon wondered if his Priestess would be an Eastern. He had heard tales of their exciting ways in the sexual ritual. His friends laughed about these stories, but none of them had been on a Pilgrimage, so Simon concluded they made it all up. Maybe there was no real sexual ritual. Maybe it was wishful thinking on the part of young boys. If there was a Priestess, would she choose him, or would he have to choose her? How would he know how to select a woman for the ritual? Would she be old and experienced or young and completely inexperienced like him?

He wondered why no one was allowed to talk about the ritual, or the Pilgrimage. He wondered why, when young men returned from their Pilgrimage they seemed to have changed, why they never spoke of it again. Simon's mind was filled with questions, questions without answers. He finally concluded that it would be easier simply to accept the unknowable and pay attention to the remainder of his trip. Distracted by his thoughts, he almost missed the next transport gate.

Simon located the next mover and stepped on. The lights directed him to the Eastern Desert Gate and he stepped off. Once more he entered a transport, fixed the belt, stowed his pack, and sat back to wait for sleep. This time he asked the attendant for a tablet and a cup of water. She smiled and said, "Certainly. I have them right here. Is there anything else you would like?" Simon shook his head and smiled back at her. She was a pretty, young woman. She slipped Simon's Card through the register at her waist and handed it back to Simon. Unconsciously he looked to see if she was wearing a wedding ring. He smiled at himself and closed his eyes thinking of Cristin. Sleep came almost at once. He wakened refreshed, excited, and aware that he had arrived at another Travel Center, aware that he had arrived at last at the edge of the Eastern Desert. He left the transport.

There was no mover in this Travel Center. People walked short distances to their gate of departure. Simon noticed that most of the travelers were young men. He saw a few Priests and Priestesses in travel garments. He saw a group of young girls with a Priestess being hurried off in another direction. Simon thought of his sisters and wondered if they had been frightened when they made their Pilgrimage. These young girls seemed to be laughing and talking with the Priestess and with each other. These girls did not seem to be afraid. A pang of homesickness hit harder than he expected. His sisters were really very good to him. They had helped with the work for his Beginning, and he had not even remembered to say thank you.

Simon found his gate of departure. He entered the last of his transports, found an empty chair and sat down. The chairs were comfortable and attendants came by with food. To his surprise he was hungry and asked for a sandwich and some juice. The desert was visible through the viewing screen. He had never been anywhere as vast or as unpopulated as this desert. At home everyone lived in the Colony. Home, jobs, services, food - everything one needed was nearby. It was all produced and distributed within the Colony. He had never seen an expanse of land without a Colony on it. He had seen sand at the Atlantic Ocean beaches, but even the deserts of America were colonized. This, the Unending Desert, was kept holy, and therefore kept unpopulated.

Simon had heard that one could turn completely around in the center of the Holy Structure and see only desert in every direction. That possibility seemed unimaginable. He felt excited. He felt brave. He could not remember any experience to compare with this. Images of his father's expression slipped through the back of his mind as he thought of the Donning. His father had whistled that little tune as he unpacked the trunk. Did all of the older men in his Colony feel as strongly about a Pilgrimage for their sons as his father seemed to? Simon's brain felt clogged with questions he felt he should have asked when he had the chance. He tried to stop thinking.

Unlike the other transports, this last transport rode over the ground like a hydroplane. It was close to the surface and had windows for viewing. He rested while he rode, and watched the desert. What could it have been like before the Last War? Again he wished he had his history journal with him. He had read that some countries had been teeming with people, that there had been disease and pestilence, famine, and even homelessness. He found it hard to believe that the ancients could have suffered such atrocities.

As he rode along, Simon found himself wondering what the

ancients would have called this distance in kilometers or miles. He found his memory flashing back to the classroom when trainers had talked about ancient modes of travel. He remembered the test questions. He remembered passing the tests. The journal said that students used to be required to compute miles per hour, but the skill now proved to be so useless that it was dropped from the training. All Simon could remember was that it had something to do with a method of calculating distance compared with time passed. Since time and distance no longer were related to each other in any critical or practical way, study of the subject was eliminated. He sighed, conscious for the first time in his young life there was a lot he did not know.

Looking around, Simon could see that all of the travelers were young men. Some wore wedding rings. He wondered if they missed their wives. He wondered if the married men took part in the sexual rituals, and he wondered if their wives minded. Simon thought of his cousin. He asked for another tablet and slept until the transport arrived at the Gate of the Last Mile.

The transport came to a smooth stop. Simon wakened, afraid to open his eyes. He opened them a bit then closed them again and waited. In this place he had imagined so many times, he would don the clothes he had so carefully packed and carried from home. From here he would walk the Last Mile to the Holy Structure. Simon took a deep breath, opened his eyes, and looked around.

Nothing could have prepared him for what he saw. There was no food room, no mover. There were no signal-lights explaining where to go. He appeared to be standing on the outer rim of an enormous tube, a section of a huge circle, which went on out of sight in both directions. As far as he could see, to his right and to his left, young men were stepping off the transport on to shiny plastine floors. Behind them stood the transports in which they had arrived.

Opposite, at least fifty meters away, stood a wall, which consisted of a series of closed doors. The doors had no handles, no windows, and no locks as far as Simon could see. Everything was white, shiny, and immaculate. Simon set down his pack and looked around at his companions. This section of the tube was filled with young men from all over the world. Even though they were all dressed in travel suits made of ecofibers, he could recognize Easterns, Africans, Westerns, Polarians, Europeans, Southerns; every known race seemed to be present. The young men stood very still. They waited. At least Simon was not the only one who did not know what to do next.

His translator began to beep. He turned the knob. The other young men stopped to adjust their wristbands. A voice came through Simon's translator: "Welcome to the Gate of the Last Mile. You will cross the corridor, enter any door in front of you. There you will bathe, then put on the relic clothing you have brought with you. You will leave your pack, your travel suits, and your Card. From here on you will need nothing you have brought with you except your relic clothing and your translator."

Simon walked to the nearest door, as did several other young men. He had never seen any of them before They all seemed as nervous as he was. For that he was grateful. The massive door slid open. The men entered. They were in an open space surrounded by lockers. It was a changing room much like a locker room at a fitness center. It looked clean and not crowded. Simon took off his travel suit and hung it in a locker. He stepped into the bathing pool, soaked in the warm water, showered off, and began to dress in the clothes he had so carefully carried with him.

Simon's clothes were fairly easy to put on. He had trouble tying the laces on the shoes but finally managed to get them to stay together. He wiggled his toes in the stiff leather shoes and glanced up at the other young men. He finished quickly with the necktie, sure he had done it wrong, and looked around at the other young men. He could see that each of them seemed to have a particular order for the Donning of his own clothes. All of the travel garments had been alike except for the color of the biofibers. Now as they completed the Donning, each young man was in the costume of his Colony, in the ancient ritual clothing of his family.

Simon's first impression was of the colorful clothing, how interesting they were compared to the suits issued by the producers. Even his own relic clothes seemed dull compared to those he saw on many of the other young men. There were sashes of many colors, strings of beads made of bone and wood and glass. Some of the young men wore trousers with full legs, billowy shirts, tight hose, and shoes of every design imaginable. He saw hats of differing styles and colors and materials.

He saw cloth he had only heard of from his great-grandmother. From the look of the patterns and colors there must have been satins, silks made by living worms, linens, which his grandmother told him were beaten from plant fiber, cottons, brocades, homespun raw wools. He realized his grandmother knew things they did not teach in school. He wondered how she had learned them.

A few of the young men wore feathers from exotic birds, furs which must have actually covered live animals, or the skins of snakes and reptiles Simon had read about at the Museum of the Ancients. Many of those species had almost been destroyed in the Last War. Simon thought they must have been beautiful and terrifying to behold when they had roamed the earth. Now, a few were kept in zoological museums for breeding purposes. Many were gone completely. He could not see enough fast enough. He wanted to ask each young man about his clothes. The endless variety of clothing and materials held his attention completely. The young men completed their Donning and then waited, unabashedly watching each other.

Simon began to wonder about the long anticipated ceremony. After the formal Donning ceremony at home, he had imagined that a Priest or Priestess would watch the men don their clothes, or music would play or something more exciting than this would happen. This was like the changing rooms at the Training Center, with all the young men in the locker-room, and pools for group bathing. One by one the men stored their travel garments and sat down on the wooden benches to wait.

No one spoke. The quiet was uncomfortable and it was difficult to keep from staring at one another. Simon was afraid the other young men would see the fear in his eyes. No one came in. No one left. After what seemed like an eternity, a voice spoke through the translators. "Please remove your foot coverings. Please come into the center. Please enter the inner doors. Here you will be fed. After you eat, you will rest. Then you will walk the Last Mile. Please come in and find a place to sit down."
The young men walked on past the lockers, past the pools, inward, through the next band of doors. This room, like the other, appeared to be a section of a long tube or tunnel. Simon could see in either direction, until the bend in the circle closed off his view.

The young men sat down at tables in groups of three or four. They had traveled from all over the earth; they had traveled for at least two days. They did not know each other. They waited in silence. Soon, young men and women arrived carrying large trays pilled high with plates of food. Food supplements and beverages arrived. No one had to ask for anything. The men ate. Simon mumbled a thank you to the Server, but she did not respond. The chairs reclined and sleep came to Simon almost immediately.

After what seemed like a very brief sleep, the translators beeped, and a voice wakened them saying, "The next door will open. You will take off your shoes and carry them. You will put on sandals from the boxes next to the doors. You will wear the cloak you brought with you to cover your heads in order to protect yourselves from the sun. You will walk the Last Mile to the Holy Structure."

Chapter 3
THE FIRST PRAYER

"…and we will leave the familiar. Cherishing memory,
we will dip our finger tips into new waters, taste, and
then decide if the world is crazed or sane."

Ohma LW355
OHMA'S WORD

As the next door opened, Simon could see the exterior walls of
the Holy Structure in the distance. Actually what he saw was
a mile of sand and only a small section of the Holy Structure,
which appeared to be round, and larger than anything he had
ever seen before. He had no way of knowing its circumference.
He had seen drawings by artists who had been allowed to fly
over the Holy Structure in primitive aircraft. No photolight
impressions had been allowed. Those who were given the
privilege could sketch as they flew and then do renderings
from memory. He was so busy craning his neck to see the Holy
Structure that he almost forgot to find a pair of sandals for
his bare feet. He rummaged around in the sandal box finally
finding a pair, which seemed to be the right length and width.
All of the sandals were made of leather, old and worn.

He could see that the Holy Structure consisted of circles within
circles, each one rising higher, taller than the one before, the

last circle surrounding a slender tower. The silvery tower in the center rose so high, was so far away, there could be no way to estimate its height. Simon pulled on his pair of sandals, pulled the hood of his robe over his head in order to shade his face. He tucked his stockings into his leather shoes, picked them up by the heels, and stepped onto the sand. He was glad the old robe covered his head and his clothes. Even though the robe dragged through the sand, it covered him completely from the burning rays of the sun.

On the first steps of this long awaited walk, the hot sand slipped into his sandals, rubbing on the soles of his feet. He wondered why the Ancients had worn sandals. They were more interesting than today's foot coverings, but did not have the molded comfort or protection. They did not seem to be cast to the shape of one's foot. It also seemed to Simon that sandals would eventually wear out. Thoughts about foot-coverings and exercise were not what he had expected as he walked the Last Mile. He had expected this walk to feel holy, perhaps saint-like, but it was simply hot and uncomfortable.

The old clothing felt odd. The sandals slipped up and down on his heels. He had not been provided with liquids for the walk. Perhaps this Pilgrimage wasn't all it was built up to be. Perhaps his father had implied it was a something special in order to cover his own disappointment. There was no way to turn back. Simon was not going to admit to his feelings in front of the other young men. He thought to himself that it must be important or the Elders would not continue to insist that every young man on earth make this hot and supposedly holy trek.

The mile seemed endless to Simon. Thirst was real for the first time in his young life. He felt hungry. He was aware of the clothes against his skin. Some of the cloth was rough and made him itch. He could see and feel a painful swelling on his heel where the sandal strap rubbed as he walked. He began to be grateful to the scientists who had developed ecofibers.

This part of the Pilgrimage didn't feel holy. It felt more like parts of the training years. Simon wondered if his companions who had already done their years of service to the Corps were faring any better than he was. Perhaps they were somehow tougher than he was. Perhaps they were not suffering these bodily discomforts. He felt a little ashamed of his feelings of discomfort, felt he should somehow not feel the way he was really feeling. Looking around, he found it difficult to determine who had done their service and who, like himself, had only recently turned old enough to serve.

He wished he had already done his two years of service. He wished he had walked many miles with his fellows in the Corps, saving lives, helping people in time of flood and fire. Perhaps then he would be stronger, more comfortable in the heat. He could not fathom the idea of the Corps having been an army, as the Trainers had explained, with different nations supporting different armies. The Trainers taught, and the journals substantiated, that men had actually fought against each other, had done bodily harm, causing pain, wounds, and very often - death. Simon could not imagine being part of such a thing.

It was impossible to imagine the men of today's Corps harming anyone. The Corps was formed and sustained in order to help in times of need, and continued to be dedicated to saving lives. Thinking about the Corps helped keep his mind off his sore feet.

Simon and all the members of his Colony were aware the Corps was necessary because scientists had still not mastered control of earthquakes, tidal waves, floods, or forest fires started by lightning. The alarm systems managed to remove most of the people from danger, but there was always the rebuilding to be done. The work done by the Corps put people back in the homes, rebuilt dikes, and made all the necessary repairs. The Corp offered medical assistance and emergency supplies. In preparation for the Corps there was always a good purpose to the things the Trainers made you do, but this walk felt like pointless trudging.

The closer Simon came to the Holy Structure, the more tension he felt. Fear, rage at the heat, pain from the sandals, sore legs from walking in deep sand, wonder at the place, awe, hope, anticipation, streaked through him in strange emotional, almost colorful, patterns.

He could just begin to see the details of the massive structure. Expansive panes of glass filled some of the archways between huge supportive timbers. The reflection off the glass was almost blinding. By putting his fingers over his eyes, he could just see that a few of the archways appeared to stand open. There was no shade in the unending desert making it hard to see very far. He trudged on. Coming closer to the outer wall, Simon's fatigue faded as his excitement increased.

Head down, still covered by his hood, he stepped through one of the arches into the shade of the Holy Structure. The desert winds had blown sand into the great, broad openings leaving shallow sandbars so deep he could not feel the floor. It was dark inside and the contrast from the brilliant reflection of the sunlight off the sand left him momentarily blind. Simon dropped his hood and felt the cool air on his head. He stepped forward until the sand under his feet gradually disappeared.

The floor consisted of dark red squares fashioned from a

material, which looked to Simon like the relic bowls made of ceramic clay. The squares were rough at the edges and uneven to walk on, as if they had been made by hand. As his eyes became accustomed to the dark, he could see the timbers, which held up the roof. Trunks of entire trees had been cut and formed into columns to support the roof. The ceiling was formed of carved wooded beams, set together in long panels.

It was true! The Holy Structure was made of all natural materials. Simon did not see one bioboard or ecofiber anywhere. He found it hard to believe there could be that many natural materials in one place, and this was only the first circle. He wondered how many circles there were, how many he would be allowed to see before his Pilgrimage ended.

As he walked deeper into the shade of the outer circle, he saw Priests and Priestesses walking among the young men who had arrived with him. The Priesthood wore robes of flowing, colored cloth, woven in wonderful rainbow colors, tied at the waist with sashes of ribbons and leather and beads. The robes looked soft and comfortable. They all wore sandals, but they walked well and did not seem to suffer as Simon had. A Priestess came up to Simon. He guessed she was close to the age of his mother. She had a kind expression and she spoke to him gently. Simon did not hear a word for the rush of questions in his head.

She spoke to Simon again, "Please follow me Simon."

"How did you know my name?" he asked. She said nothing.

This time he followed, and she led him to a group of young men. The young men were talking animatedly with an older Priest. Some were asking the questions, some were adjusting their translators, some talked with each other. As the Priestess walked up to the group, the Priest hushed the others and waited for her to speak. She was friendly and informal. She asked, "Are any of you hungry or thirsty? Do you have blisters on your feet from the sandals? There is balm and tape for them if they hurt." She seemed altogether a kind and motherly woman. Simon was no longer afraid, just curious.

One young man said, "I am very thirsty." Clay water bottles were produced from a cart. Simon looked at the other men. He assumed they too were trying to assess what they were feeling. He wondered if they could be as excited as he was.

The Priestess spoke several dialects, and she talked with the young men answering their questions as she strolled along. As their eyes became more accustomed to the dark shade inside the Holy Structure, they could begin to see the details of this place he had imagined so often. Each section of the building was fitted into the next. Simon had seen the joining work his father had done in keeping his Craft of woodworking, but he had never imagined that entire buildings could be fitted together and held in place with notches and hard pegs made of black metal.

The buildings at home in his Colony were assembled with a plastine mortar, each section of the room fitting into the next. An entire house could be assembled in less than a week, and occupied the next when the solar generators were connected. Simon thought to himself that the Holy Structure must have taken thousands of craftsmen many thousands of days to build.

Simon heard the Priestess say something about "under construction for more than five hundred years." He came sharply to attention and adjusted his translator; he did not want to miss any more of her explanation. She went on to say,

"After the Last War the great cities of the Unending Desert had been destroyed. The people had to wait for many years before they dared try to live in this part of the world, before it was safe even to breathe the air."

She continued: "All life had been killed. Great rivers stopped running, their paths changed when the earthquakes came after the underground explosions. The Unending Desert would never grow anything again, even if the water could be made to flow."

The young men walked in silence unable to take in the meaning of what she was saying. She went on, "Food grown here now grows in the greenhouse circle with water collected during the rainstorm season, stored, recycled, and used as needed. We also pump from a few very deep springs for drinking water." This was the first time Simon heard a reference to another circle. His curiosity moved faster than his understanding.

One of the young men smiled at the Priestess and said, "You remind me of my mother. Will you be my Priestess for the sexual ritual?"

Simon looked away, embarrassed. The woman smiled, laughed a warm-hearted laugh but did not answer the question. She reached out and gave his shoulder a pat. The young man, no more than eighteen, blushed, but he was not offended, as the Priestess was so kind.

She slipped her arm around the embarrassed young man's shoulder, and went on with her story about the Holy Structure.

"The people who colonized the Unending Desert decided to build the structure of all natural materials. It was not called the Holy Structure at first. At first it was to be a tribute to the world of nature, which had been so damaged, so decimated. It was also a way to make sure the ancient Crafts were not lost to an info-scientific society, not lost as the people who were left searched for new ways to provide for their needs. Wood was hauled, nails were forged from iron, glass was made from sand, arches built from stone, tiles made of clay, roof tiles formed over the thighs of the craftsmen. Everything was made the old way when the Holy Structure was first built. And yes, all additions and repairs are still done the same way." She paused.

One of the young men asked the Priestess a question; "Did the Last War really kill half of the earth's population?"

She did not answer him directly. She went on to say, "The original work on the Holy Structure was done by men. The workmanship was superb because the workers were so glad to be alive that they treasured the right to work and to do that work carefully."

Another of Simon's companions asked, "Where were the women? Could any of them have babies?"

She answered, "Some of the women bore children and were needed to attend to those children, and rest of the women needed to study means of survival. In the early days, the Holy Structure was no larger than a Colony Museum."

She went on, "Fully half of the women who survived the Last War could not carry a child because of the radiation damage, so they prepared to study what they needed to know in order for people to survive at all. Women have always been interested in survival you know."

She smiled at the young men and went on, "The women

became the scholars, the survivalists, the scientists. They developed ways to grow food with a minimum of water, to make medicines from plants, to reach the healing parts of the mind in order to cure and prevent disease."

"How could they do all that and take care of the children?" asked another young man, a dark skinned man with a bright bead hanging from his left ear. Simon had never seen a man wear beads, or earrings. As he watched the young man with the earring, his mind began to wander. So much was completely new to Simon.

The Priestess answered, "Those women who could carry a child did so. No one knew for sure how many of those born, would live, or be able to reproduce. Life became possible here. Life was treasured here, as it is today. Gradually this place came to be called The Holy Structure. It became evident to some of the leaders that the young people of the earth must visit at least once in their lives. They needed to see how the ancient Crafts were kept intact, how natural materials once provided for the good of the people, how people had survived for generations without the new ways."

As she spoke, these young men from different parts of the world began to look at each other more carefully, to examine the use of natural materials, which they wore on their bodies. The Priestess now spoke in an ancient dialect, but they connected the earpiece of their translators, making it possible for them to understand her story. Another young man from the Africas asked, "What were the people in the rest of the world doing while this structure was being built?"

She went on, "Each country's army was the segment of the society best prepared for survival. If there was food, medicine, or supplies, the armies held them. The armies had the best-stocked shelters. At first the leaders of the armies continued to talk about such irrelevant topics as 'winning' and 'flags' and 'superior weapons'. Some of the men actually continued to plan for wars, which they thought they could win, in which they imagined they would capture the goods and supplies of another army."

The men looked puzzled. One fair skinned man said, "But then there would not be enough to go around."

The Priestess smiled and went on to say, "Boundaries had become meaningless. There was no nationalized economic structure left, no way to make currency. There were no functioning governments. Most of the world's gold, which men valued highly, was melted into great blobs of metal and cement inside the various national vaults. Actually, the idea of winning or losing had become meaningless. So much had to be rethought and unlearned." She looked thoughtful and waited for what she had said to be received, to be taken in, even if it was not fully understood.

She went on," During all this time, the women were carrying babies when they could and studying from those books, which were not destroyed. Many of the libraries and universities, being of little value in war, were left standing. Those institutions whose libraries were underground still had books and pictures in good condition. The women formed study groups, built study centers. Later the women, with the help of the men of course, built laboratories, universal learning centers, and communication systems."

The Priestess went on with her history of what had occurred after the Last War. All of the women's endeavors had the same goal, to make sure the planet could and would survive. "After long periods of time, science-industries were created to provide people with the basic necessities of life. Both men and women worked. They produced only what people really needed to survive and reproduce. It seemed foolish to produce anything which would waste precious resources."

The young men listened in silence. Now, they did not ask questions. They could not absorb all they had heard. A Priest at the back of the group said, "I think it is time to eat." At the thought of food Simon was suddenly hungry. He had forgotten the long walk, the thirst. The Priestess again asked them to follow her. This time Simon heard and paid attention.

The corridor to the food hall was hung with paintings and drawings depicting the old ways, the old Crafts. One picture showed a man dressed in an apron made of leather, forging small nails with a hammer. Another drawing showed a man driving a nail into a board to hold it in place next to another board. In the painting this task was done with a kind of hammer unlike any Simon's father had in his shop. The tools and methods shown in the pictures seemed endless in their variety, all requiring skill and hard labor. The ancients must have been very strong. Simon had heard stories of how they wore out easily, how they only lived about seventy-five years.

They came to a great hall where food was brought to the young men by a group of men and women dressed like the ones who had served them before. The Priestess said, "These young men and women are called Servers." Simon took a closer look at them. A majority of the Servers were young women. Some were young men. The Priestess went on saying, "These young men and women have chosen service and the Priesthood for their life's work."

The Servers seemed relaxed and comfortable. They spoke the old dialect but many could speak in several languages.

They visited with the young men, laughing easily at their need for translators. They walked easily in their robes and sandals. Simon knew that anyone could apply to become a Priest or Priestess. He also knew that only a few, very select, men and women were chosen. If chosen, it would be a life of dedication.

The Servers seemed to move with ease and grace. They smiled easily too and they seemed to be content. It wasn't that they were particularly pretty or handsome, rather that they seemed happy and generous in spirit. Simon noticed one young woman, how her hair moved when she walked. He wondered if one of these would be with him in the sexual ritual. His heart took a gentle leap. He had to stop thinking about it.

The food was delicious. The Priestess went on with her explanations: "All of the food you will eat while you are here is produced in the Holy Structure, all grown in the greenhouse circle. The fruits and vegetables, the grains, the soy beans, goat cheese, are all prepared here in kitchens with wood stoves, cooked in clay and iron vessels. These cooking vessels are made here. They are newer versions of the relics you used at home for your Beginning."

Simon's mother had made porridge, with lumps, once in her life. These cooks made food for all the young men on earth, and it was wonderful, delicious food. No supplements were offered after the meal. Simon had heard that the food grown here needed no supplements. This food could actually nourish the body completely. He was going to ask if that was so, but he was too tired. The voices around him were fading. As much as he wanted to hear every word the Priestess spoke, fatigue limited his capacity to hear, and his ability to understand was fading.

He heard the Priestess say, "It will soon be time for bed." She smiled at the young men who had come so far this day. Simon was almost asleep as he sat listening and nodding. She told them, "Rest on the sleep-mats, which you will find on the floor against the inner wall. Remove and store your clothing. Wear the robes, which hang on the pegs against the wall."

Simon was too tired to worry about sleeping garments, too tired to be concerned about tomorrow. He took off his clothes, slipped into a robe, leaving his precious garments in a pile on the floor next to his mat. In the distance he heard a voice reminding them to pray their first Life Prayer before sleep.

Simon realized he had forgotten to plan his Seven Life Prayers while he traveled. Annoyed with himself, but too sleepy to care, he did remember that he didn't want Cristin to find another man while he was away on his service to the Corps. It seemed irrelevant now, but he mumbled his first prayer into the close darkness, then he slept.

Chapter 4
SECOND PRAYER

"Our bodies come from the earth, are fed by the earth,
return to the earth. Let the love of our bodies be
as natural, strong, yielding, and fruitful as the earth."

Woong Su of the East LW1203
WOONG SU'S WRITINGS

The day began with a loud gonging of bells, with the shuffle
of sandals, with delicious aromas of food, with voices talking
softly, and with the sound of laughter. It might have been a
holiday at home, but there were no signs of anything special
or festive. Priests, Priestesses, and Servers seemed to be going
about the natural business of their day.

Simon awoke to the voice of a Priest, "Young men, it is time
to get up, to wash in the basins by the tables, and to come to
the tables for food." Simon obeyed. Sleepy-eyed, he washed,
dressed, and went to the tables. He didn't remember the tables
from the night before.

The tables were made of great slabs of wood worn to a smooth
ripe glow over many years of use. The grain of the great planks
drew beautiful patterns much like the pictures of ancient maps
Simon had seen in the Colony Museum. The benches were

hard, without cushions, but the warm wood felt comfortable against his body. He remembered the morning of his Beginning and how the banister his father had fashioned felt warm under his hand. The porridge served in clay bowls smelled of grains and honey. It was hot. No lumps. Large platters of sliced fresh fruits sat in the middle of the table, each platter holding a metal fork for serving the fruit. The woven cloth napkins showed wear, some with a threadbare place or two. Relics seemed commonplace here at the Holy Structure. The ancient ways seemed strange to Simon, but gentle and flexible, able to change with time.

After breakfast the Priest asked the group of young men to follow him to the next inner circle. The young men left the residue of their meal behind. Simon heard the Servers humming and chatting while they cleared and washed the tables. He wondered if the Servers were pleased with their life choice. During training he had studied about times when there had been distinct social classes in society. Some people had actually made their way in the world by serving other people. There had even been a time when groups of people were slaves, and were owned by other people. Simon had never seen anyone like the Servers, people doing other people's work for them.

The Servers did not seem to mind serving others. They seemed joyful. He wondered if the Servers were owned, or paid a wage. Here they seemed to work for others because they wanted to. Simon did not know of anyone at home who did anyone else's work. At home in the Colony every person did their own work, and every person received what they needed to live well.

The Priest led the young men across more of the ceramic tiles, under heavy beamed ceilings, down a long stone corridor lit only by flaming torches set in iron holders in the rock. Going deeper and deeper into the Holy Structure, he led them through another set of tall arches like those they had passed through after the Last Mile. As they walked under the thick arches the tile floor ended. Gravel had been spread in a wide circle, and from the outer circumference, paths led into a wood. In this circle the desert had been transformed into a wild garden, the burning sun of the Endless Desert shut out by many layers of glass ceiling. Trees had been planted, streams created. Plants dotted the land and small animals wandered free. Birds sang, insects hummed. Life here was thriving and energetic.

The young men sat down on a cool patch of grass by a stream and waited for the Priest to tell them of the next step. The Priest simply sat and rested with them. No one said anything at all. Simon sat very still and listened to the birds. He had never heard so many different bird songs.

One of the young men, to Simon he looked like a Northern, asked the Priest, "How should I decide what to pray for in my Life Prayers?"

The Priest said, "It really doesn't matter, as all life is a prayer." The young Northern looked puzzled and did not ask again. Simon did not understand what he meant either, but it didn't seem to matter, and he would have been embarrassed to ask for an explanation.

Simon thought about his prayers and tried to decide what he would pray for that night. He had no idea how to decide what the seven most important needs of his life might be. He felt totally unprepared for such decisions. He had no criteria, no way to decide. He felt a little annoyed and more than a little frustrated. He decided to decide later. The Priest said, "You will be left here for a while alone." Then he went away. The young men sat and waited looking at the water and the woods. They couldn't help but sneak quick looks at each other.

Soon a young male Server came into the garden and asked one of the young men to go along one of the wooded paths with him. The young man went along with the Server without even asking where he was going. The rest of the young men waited quietly. Later a young woman Server came in and asked another young man to go with her. They went down one of the many paths into the woods and were not seen again. Perhaps it was the bird song or the quiet calm, but no one seemed to be afraid.

Simon wandered by the water, listening for forest sounds. About an hour later, a girl Server came to Simon and took his hand. She smiled but did not say a word. Simon got up slowly from the grass, brushed off his robe and went with her. The girl led Simon along a path to a deep shadowed pool in the stream. They did not speak. Simon did not know where he was going and it seemed pointless to care.

The young woman seemed completely at ease. She sat by the water's edge, smiled, and patted the grass for Simon to sit next to her. They sat a long while by the water. She slipped her sandals off and put her feet in the stream letting the water play with her toes. Laughing gently, she watched Simon. Simon slipped off his sandals and put his feet in the water. A small fish nibbled on his toes. He laughed aloud. The girl slipped her robe off her shoulders, let it fall to the ground in a tumbled pile, and slipped into the pool. The fish scurried away. The quiet girl bent over in the water and nibbled on Simon's toes. She looked into his eyes and said, "There is nothing to be afraid of." Simon was not afraid. He wondered why she spoke.

When Simon awakened it was almost dark. The girl must have put her robe over his naked body. She was nowhere to be seen. He was alone in the woods and Simon felt a flash of fear for the first time since he had entered the Holy Structure. There had not been any sexual ritual. What had happened between them was as natural as breathing. Simon felt suddenly calm. The girl would be back, or perhaps she wouldn't. He felt the fear again.

He wondered why no one ever spoke about this part of the Pilgrimage. He wondered if he should have done this before the sexual ritual. What if he had ruined some part of his Pilgrimage? He would ask her when she returned. If she returned.

He thought about touching her. Touching her was warm and cool and hot all at the same time. She had not taught him anything. They simply did what they wanted to do. She had cried out in pleasure, so had Simon. He had not felt self-conscious or afraid. Could this have been the ritual the boys whispered about back at the Colony?

When the girl did return, she was naked. Her fair skin was radiant in the night air. She stooped and pulled the robe from Simon's naked body and lowered herself down over him, her hair loose on his face. She sat on him and leaned back. He watched her nipples tighten and lift. The smell of her was sweeter than the flowers, the sound of her breathing, sweeter than the bird song.

Later she curled up next to him and they slept. Some time in the darkest night she kissed his body. He returned the kisses. They tasted each other. She teased him with fern and moss. She hid from him in the water and tried to climb out over the bank, but Simon swam up behind her as she held on to a tangled tree root. He pulled her back and she pressed against him.

At dawn she sat leaning against a fallen tree sucking on a reed, her robe loose about her. The glow of first light bathed her body. He leaned forward against the tree and took the reed from her mouth with his lips. He gently nibbled her lips.

In the late afternoon as the light faded from the trees they walked back out of the woods, stopping at a nurselog to love one more time. She sat astride the end of the log and leaned back. Simon felt as though he entered her, and the tree, and the earth. They walked back to the clearing together. She spoke again, "I will be leaving you now. I am sure you must be hungry. Please join the others." She said nothing more and walked into the woods down the same path from which they had returned.

Blankets had been spread on the grass by stream. Picnic baskets sat by the blankets and the young men helped themselves to food. Simon sat on the edge of one of the blankets. He was hungry. He hadn't realized how hungry he was. He presumed the girl had gone off to help with the food. He looked around for her, hoping she would share the basket of food with him.

When the food was eaten and the remains put away, a Priest asked the men to follow him. They were led to the edge of the wood where a large open sided hall had been floored and made comfortable with tables and chairs. Each table was centered with a bowl of fresh wild flowers and ferns. Servers came with steaming pots of green tea, small bowls, and wooden dishes of almond cakes.

This evening the young men were laughing and talking with the Servers, some using their translators, some just laughing at the mistakes they made in their attempts to communicate, some gesturing wildly. Simon looked again and again for the girl, but he did not see her. Once he thought he saw her, but she was sitting with another young man. Simon looked away troubled by the feelings choking in his throat. He took a deep breath and did not look back.

Simon wondered if any of the other young men had been worried about a sexual ritual. He was much too self-conscious to ask if there was such an event at all. Perhaps the whole idea had been a fantasy created in the imaginations of excited and frightened young men. Thoughts of his cousin Cristin came and went as he remembered the lovely Server girl in the wood. He found himself wondering how many Pilgrims his Server had initiated into the wonders of making love. He began to think about the term - making love. He began to think about why the Elders taught the Rules of Fidelity, why married couples took vows of constancy. His Second Life Prayer was beginning to take form somewhere in the back of his mind.

Chapter 5
THIRD PRAYER

"Until we understand how inhumane,
how hideous we can be,
we will never come fully into the light, never
fully understand our true choices."

Green Grass the First LW23
THE PEACE JOURNALS

When an Elder Priestess came to the tables and told the young men to follow her to the next circle, Simon did not want to go. He looked around the hall, but he could not find the sweet girl Server whose memory would not leave his mind. For a moment he thought she passed by with a tray on her shoulder, but when he took a better look he was not sure it really was her. The Servers all seemed to look similar when they wore their robes and were busy working at their tasks.

A quiet young Server brushed his shoulder with her breasts as she gathered the food things. Simon felt calm and he wanted to find the other girl and return to the garden.

The Elder Priestess insisted they finish the last of their tea then said, "You will be led by another Priestess through the next door." The woman entered and waited by the door until they were finished eating. They followed and found themselves back walking on sand.

Simon pulled the hood of his robe over his head, welcoming the dark privacy for his private, intimate thoughts, and followed the tall, older woman. She was the only person here who had told them her name. When they were gathered at the last doorway she said simply, "My name is Green Grass. I am named for an early Priestess. As an Elder Priestess I was able to choose my own name after leaving life in the Colonies." She made no further explanation. She seemed to Simon to be deeply sad. She led them through the sand to a gravel path, along the path to a wooden house. The house was set low against the ground. The outer walls of this unusual house were fashioned of rectangular paper screens held in place by strips of honey colored wood.

They were led around the house to a small, octagonal stone building with an open doorway. As they passed through the arch they entered a room containing deep tubs of steaming water and benches holding soap bars, towels and small buckets of hot water. Green Grass directed the young men to wash their bodies thoroughly using the soap and small buckets of water before entering the basins where they could soak and rest before bed.

The men did as they were told. As he sat in the deep wooden tub, Simon found that he was more rested than he had been since he had left home. Green Grass returned, instructed them, saying, "Please dry with the clean stacked towels, then dress in the cotton robes you will find folded on your sleeping mats." She went on, "The mats will be found inside the house we just passed." Simon had a sudden moment of panic; he could not recall what had happened to the relic clothing he had brought from home.

The young men clambered out of the water when it finally grew too cool to enjoy. They dried off and walked naked back to the screened house. A Server slid back one of the screens to expose a bare floor spread with rush mats. The night air was warm. Simon unfolded the robe at the foot of one mat. Lying down on the mat, he was surprised to find it comfortable. He was soon asleep.

In the morning Servers arrived with tea, fruit, and bread. The young men ate in silence. This serene, still place did not encourage talk. The usual clutter of daily living was missing. A single stem of blossoms stood in a slender glass vase set in a niche in the only stone wall of this otherwise empty room. They waited in silence. By now Simon knew that he did not have to make decisions. He had simply to follow the next set of orders given him. In this remarkable place, he could not imagine what he might do unless told. Green Grass returned and asked, "Will you all please follow me." Again, in silence they followed.

They crossed a broad sandy patch and headed even further in toward the center of the Holy Structure. Where the sand ended, gravel began, small gravel, neatly raked. Here and there were small, seat-sized stones placed in groups around larger, stones, which stood as tall as a man. They walked on round stones set in a curved path through the raked gravel. It took concentration and care to stay on the flagstone pathway. When finally he looked up, Simon saw a craggy stone wall centered by a wooden gate. The men passed single file through the gate, bending their heads to clear the low overhead beam.

Simon entered a garden unlike any he had ever seen. The young man from the East cried out, saying something Simon did not understand. The young man, an Eastern, obviously took pleasure in what he saw. Simon remembered the sounds of pleasure he and the Server had made in the garden of the wild wood. He shook his head to force the memories away.

Here, unlike the woods, was laid a careful garden, a meticulous garden. The small, ancient trees stood like sculptures. One bamboo stalk carried a small stream of water, which dripped from the end, making music as it fell into a stone basin. The pathways, steep and irregular, turned at sharp angles, presenting with each twist another scene of peace and quiet.

As they came to a high, crimson, arched bridge by a curved, stone rimmed pool filled with colorful fish, Green Grass stopped. She spoke: "This garden has been chosen as the way to The Pictures of The End of The Earth. It was chosen because it represents a country once known as Japan, the first place on Earth where nuclear arms were exploded in an act of war. The buildings in the garden, which you will soon visit, show drawings and paintings of the history of primitive nuclear weapons. They also show the pictures of the development of these weapons and the nature of the damage they do."

She went on, "We have chosen the contrast between the Japanese garden and the pictures to help you develop a thorough understanding of mankind's choices. Ancient men could have spent their time creating such gardens, or they could produce the weapons you will see. You are free to spend the rest of the day in the gardens as long as you visit all of the buildings and look at all of The Pictures of The End of The Earth. You may not go on with your Pilgrimage until you have viewed all of The Pictures of The End of The Earth. You will please remove your sandals before entering any of the buildings."

Green Grass stood tall and straight, then let her robe fall from her shoulders. Her left breast was missing. A tattoo ran across her body, shaped like a long scar, it ran from her right shoulder through to her left hipbone. It looked like both a burn and a cut. Simon turned his head so he would not have to look at the scar. Green Grass pulled her robe around her and walked quietly away. She made no explanation.

Simon glanced around at the gardens. He remembered the breasts of the lovely young Server who had spent the night with him. He yearned for her tender young body. A quick vision of the scar on Green Grass' body flashed through his mind. Dizzy, he walked to the nearest bench and sat down. In front of him was a deep green pool, formed by a curve in the pond. Koi swam lazily in and out of the lily pads. He did remember from Training that these gold and silver fish were called Koi. He did not know there were any Koi left on earth. The fish swam under the wooden bridge, turned with a flash of color and tail, and then came back to his side of the pool.

The tree next to where Simon sat was as thick in the trunk as he was. The top of the tree was shaped and trimmed. The reflection in the water was a perfect view of a miniature ancient tree. Simon could see that the tree must have been carefully planned and tended for many generations.

On the far side of the bridge stood a small wood framed building, the walls made of translucent paper screens. Like the room where he had slept, the screens slid open to reveal mats on the floor. He could see from the bench where he sat, the interior walls were hung with drawings and pictures of many sizes. Simon rose and walked slowly and carefully across one of the high, arched bridges and entered the building. He looked at the pictures.

The first picture appeared to be a photolight impression showing a wall, which reflected the images of bones, no people, just the reflection of human bones. The next picture showed a face with the eyeballs melting, running down the cheeks of what might have been a young woman. The next depicted buildings, twisted and fallen, barren land with no living thing in sight, black clouds covering the horizon. A white and gray cloud in the shape of a giant mushroom filled one picture, which covered an entire wall. Small pictures gathered together, making a collage of tattered and burned toys. Simon saw where there had been gaping holes in the earth, riverbeds with no rivers, rows of charred antique vehicles, deep grave ravines with bones and rotting flesh.

One picture after another covered the wooden partitions: hideous scenes of hospital rooms packed tight with people. Pictures of old people with arms and legs missing, food covered with flies and insects, pictures of people with blackened bodies standing where dwellings had been. The horrors went on and on. Bodies lying part in and part out of a river of running water. Gray rain on black soil. Simon tried to walk a straight line, tried to walk out into the garden without falling. There had been no explanation written beside the pictures. He did not know what they could possibly have been said to explain the content.

In his head, Simon had an image of the words printed in the study books used in Training. He vaguely remembered something like, "…after the Last War it took many years to document the destruction. One of the problems with the documentation was caused by the fact that the researchers could not tolerate the work for prolonged periods of time…" The clash between those seemingly harmless words read in Training, and the reality of the visions here in the garden drove a wedge, a split, through his consciousness, a split he could not resolve.

Simon felt violently ill, but could not vomit. His body filled with pain. Shooting pains ran down his back and up his neck until he felt as if his head would come off. He wished it would. He put one hand on top of his head, one under his chin. He sat still. Suffering. When he felt safe to let go of his head, he rested his hands on his lap. He realized that there were three more buildings to go. This would be a very long day. He wondered if any young man had ever been unable to complete his Pilgrimage.

Simon decided to walk through more of the garden before facing another of the seemingly delicate Japanese structures. He had never seen such suffering. He had heard of war, disease, pestilence, deformity, but he had never seen it. The Trainers did not feel it necessary to put such things in the textbooks and manuals. Old, thick books, and microfilms about the history of war were deep in the basement of the library to be used only by women scholars of antiquity. The Trainers had told him about them. Simon had so many questions, and yet, somehow, he did not want to know the answers.

The gardens became steeper, the paths more rocky. The splash of water falling from stone bowls, worn deep over the years, wet the stairs here and there. The plants, like sculpture, appeared to have grown to an intentional beauty. Simon sat on another bench trying to concentrate on a reflecting pool. He had to close his eyes against the beauty around him.

When finally, he could open his eyes, he realized he had to go on. It had been made clear that no young man could complete his Pilgrimage without viewing the rest of The Pictures of the End of the Earth. He was horrified at the idea that he was actually sitting in this garden, considering the possibility of turning back, of not finishing what he had come here to do.

At the end of the next path, which crossed the water in a series of stone slabs, he could see another wooden building. He sat for a while, waiting to be ready, but he knew deep inside it was not possible to be ready.

Simon rose from the bench, stretched to ease his spine, and walked to the second building. This time he was not alone. As he stepped onto the matting, he saw a young man from the East sitting in front of a life sized sculpture. Simon seemed to recall this young Eastern at the changing place. Now, the young Eastern sat staring at the sculpture. Simon recalled that the Eastern man had worn clothing made from the same designs and materials as those now on the statue of the maiden before him.

The young Eastern sat on the floor, his legs crossed, his head in his hands, weeping in heavy sobs. The marble sculpture in front of him portrayed a maiden in an ancient Japanese kimono. Each fold of her kimono draped to the floor, the flowers in the carved cloth were raised. She cupped a chrysanthemum in her hand. Where her face should have been, the sculptor had dug out a blackened hollow.

The next room contained only a few drawings and three statues. The drawings seemed to be the first stages, the working designs for the carvings, showing line and pattern of cloth, folds, and prints. Three drawings attempted a face for the maiden. The artist finally abandoned the face altogether.

There was another adult size figure, this one of a man, a laborer. He carried heavy baskets of fishes on a pole over his shoulders, his body cruelly bent and broken from the weight of his toil, his face horribly disfigured and repulsively patched. His left eyelid was sewn down, his eyeball missing. He had half a nose. He could not contain the contents of his mouth, as his lips

57

were gone. The artist had tried to sketch the heat and flame, which had caused this atrocity and had given up as with the face of the maiden.

The last of the statues depicted a small child, or what was left of a small child. The infant was lying on the ground, nude. Both arms were gone from his body, one lay by his side. One leg was partly gnawed, the other, gone. A foot, a leg bone, and a heap of excrement lay beside the figure. A dog was chewing the boy's testicles, the penis already gone. Simon felt the vomit rise again. He ran from the building. He could not throw up. The garden was too beautiful. There was no place set aside for vomit. He swallowed, leaned against a stone arch and felt his gorge rise. His body was on fire. Pains shot through his muscles. His fingers ached. His brain felt as if it would explode. He needed to urinate, but there was no place for that either.

He did not know how long he had been standing there, but when he came to awareness again it was almost evening. A cool breeze drifted over the water moving the lilies and reeds. The image of the girl Server flashed through his mind. He shut it out. He did not want her memory mixed with the revulsion he felt in this place.

He walked quickly to the next building, walked through examining each detail. This time his brain and body were cool and reserved. He felt able to face whatever they had to show. Everything he saw was more than repulsive; it was intolerable. Every picture was an image of the horrors of the ancient wars. These works of art had come to be called The Pictures of The End of The Earth. But the Earth had not ended. Simon wondered just how near the ancient people had come to total annihilation.

As darkness fell, a Priest came to the garden. He herded the young men to a sleeping room. Simon did not remember where he had walked, or even if he had eaten. It didn't matter. Sleep was a drug. Sleep was a balm. Sleep was a temporary death. Simon had no question what this night's Life Prayer would be. If the choices were gardens or war...

Simon slept.

Chapter 6
THE FOURTH PRAYER

"A safe world for man-and-womankind depends on
each person's expression of a dedicated, sacrificial,
humane concern for all other persons."

Mari Mari: African LW217
FIRST WORLD LEADERSHIP
INAUGURAL ADDRESS

Simon awoke in the morning, having slept a long, black sleep.
Remembering what he had seen the day before, he sat on the
edge of his cot and wept. Looking up, he realized he was not
alone. The other young men who were awake were lying in their
covers shaking with sobs. Two or three had not wakened yet.
They were yet to cry. For the first time Simon felt a brotherly
closeness with the other young men. The fact that they could
not speak the same language did not seem to matter. Somehow
they were now connected, had become friends, and unashamed
of their tears. Simon began to wonder what kind of man could
remember such atrocities and not weep.

He looked around the room at the other young men, so like
himself, except for the color of their skin or texture of their
hair. Words Simon had only heard about, words like *prejudice*
and *bigotry* rolled around in the back of his mind. He tried

to imagine what it could have been like when people were valued based on the color of their skin or hair, or anyone of those accidental qualities of birth. He wondered if any young man was ever turned away from completing his Pilgrimage. He wondered what shame he would bring to his family and Colony if he were not allowed to complete the journey. What would happen to a young man who did not cry at the memory of the Pictures of The End of The Earth? What kind of a man would that person become? Would he have to go back to view the pictures again?

The young men sat quietly on their cots. The last three wakened, remembered the sights they had seen only yesterday, and wept. Those who were done with their tears touched their companions, embraced, and took each other's hands. When their weeping ended, they sat in a new kind of silence. They began to wonder about each other. Where had they come from? Who made the clothes they wore that first day? How were the clothes made and of what fibers?

Simon wondered if people had to suffer together in order to become friends. He shook his head at the kind of thoughts he had in this place, thoughts he had no reason to think at home in the bosom of his family, in his familiar Colony. He started to speak to another young man, but hesitated, without knowing what there was to say. He had forgotten they did not speak the same language.

The young man from the Africas had worn beads made of glass. Not the plain, clear glass Simon was familiar with, but colored glass. Simon had seen colored glass only once, in the window of an Ancient Holy Building. The African glass beads were round and had holes so that many could be strung together. They clicked, making a pleasant sound. Simon wondered if the girl for the African man was a dark beautiful color like the man. He wondered if it mattered. Simon looked at his own skin carefully for the first time. It seemed to him that he was a rather uninteresting color compared to the warm sienna of the African and the smooth, yellow-brown skin of the men from the East. He ran his fingers over the back of one hand, thinking about his skin. The skin on the back of his hands had spots his mother called 'freckles'. He had never thought about before.

A Priest entered. He was not wearing his robes. If he had not been wearing his medallion, his symbol of Priesthood, he would be unrecognizable as a Priest at all. He wore cloth made to look like patches of dark, light, and shade. He wore snug fitting, black leather gloves. He wore weapons strapped to his body, a large knife sheathed on his hip, two guns strapped to his back. Simon had seen guns used to dispense tranquilizing agents when dangerous animals had to be moved from a park to a reserve. The Priest wore a strap holding pointed tubes; it ran from the right shoulder to left hip as the tattoo on Green Grass had run. His foot coverings were tall, almost to the knee, and laced with thin straps. His expression sad, his face held the same look Green Grass had when she turned to leave them in the Japanese garden.

The Priest gave the men clothing and tall foot-coverings like his. He gave them gloves, and black head coverings, which allowed only the eyes, nose, and mouth to show. He said, "Leave your robes here. They will be safe here on the cots. The Servers will launder them while you are gone." He left.

Simon wondered where they were going, but he had learned to wait. The men dressed, fumbling with buttons and laces. The cloth was rough against their bodies. When they were all dressed, they looked at one another. In these clothes they all looked alike. Hair color and skin tones didn't show. They laughed at how much alike they looked and spontaneously started to stomp around the room together, their boots banging on the wood floor.

The Priest returned and shouted' "Be quiet! Choose one of your ranks to be your leader." He left without telling them how to choose a leader, or what the leader must do.

Of the seven young men, two were dark-skinned, one from the North was fair, Simon was a middling-fair, the two men from the South were a warm brown color, and the Eastern a yellow-brown. Simon found the colors of skin beautiful. They differed in body type, height, and weight. They differed in many ways, but for the uniforms. It was rather like wearing the biosuits they had all arrived in, but not as familiar, nor as comfortable. They had grown accustomed to seeing each other in their ancient native garments or in colored robes. They were surprised at the loss of individuality the uniform produced.

The Priest returned again and asked if they had chosen a leader. They had forgotten. The Priest left again. They had no idea how to choose a leader. They stood and stared at each other. In the Colonies, if a leader was needed, it was usually a woman.

Finally one of the Africans stepped forward, bowed deeply, hopped from one leg to another in a little dance then he jumped up on a chair. The men turned up their translators and the African explained, "I have seen pictures of native Chiefs from the ancient tribes of my family. They do this kind of dance. This must be what a leader does." They all laughed and agreed that he was as good as any. At least he was willing. When the Priest returned one more time, one of the men said, "He is our choice for leader." The Priest took the young African away without a word.

The young men sat again in silence. This was getting tiresome. They fidgeted with their laces, tugged at the shirts, opened and closed the buttons, and after what seemed like a very long time, the door opened. The African entered. He did not look at them. He sat. He stood. He stared at the ceiling, then at the wall. Finally he said something into his translator. The men listened. He said, "Check your translators and strap on your communicators. The communicators are in the left chest pocket of your uniforms." They did as they were told. As he spoke, Simon noticed that the expression in his eyes became darker. He had changed. He was no longer with them in spirit.

Their new leader ordered them to follow him as he walked out of the next set of doors and on to another broad strip of sand. He told them to walk in a single line. They trudged over the hot sand for at least an hour, no hood to shade their eyes, no water. Quite suddenly the sand ended and they faced the tree-wall of a dense and tangled jungle. The African shouted, "You are to do as I say without asking any questions. Strap on your guns and knives. The bullets are waiting in heavy wooden boxes at the edge of the jungle. Throw a strap of bullets over your shoulder." They did exactly as they were told.

Silent, the men followed their leader into the jungle, walking single file on a narrow, rough path. Walking the jungle was steamy and uncomfortable. The boots were better to walk in than sandals, but they rubbed on the heel and at the top where the leather hit the calf muscle. The weapons were heavy and the straps wore on their bodies through their shirts. Simon felt unbalanced, weighted down, and miserable. Suddenly the African stopped. Each man bumped into the man in front of him. They mumbled apologies and shifted from foot to foot. The leader shouted again, "Be quiet! NOW! "

The leader took one bullet from the strap, placed it in the gun and fired at a tree nearby. The bullet entered the trunk leaving a gaping hole in the bark. The noise was deafening. He fired again at a branch, at anything he saw, whether he could hit his target or not. He was no marksman. Explosion after explosion filled their heads. Leaves fell, branches hung, dirt flew - all random shots. There was no purpose to this. The leader told them to form a circle with their backs to each other. He walked around the ring and showed each one how to put a bullet in his gun. He hollered, "Shoot at anything you want."

The tall pale man from the North had been through his service. He had handled weapons needed to remove bears and a few other wild animals to safe compounds. The guns he had known only shot tranquilizing medicines. He said to the leader, "I cannot shoot without a reason. It is dangerous and I will not do it."

The leader told him again, "Shoot!" Again the Northern refused. The African leader pointed his gun at the Northern and the Northern began to raise his rifle, pointing it back at the leader. Then he aimed the rifle away from the leader, carefully choosing his target and hitting it. Each time he shot, he hit his target. He picked off a leaf from a high branch, cut off a small twig at the end of a limb, made a pattern of holes down the center of a broad leaf. Soon the others stopped whispering and began to watch him. Obviously it required skill to shoot a gun. They had never seen anyone shoot like this before.

The leader spoke again, "Strap on your guns and walk in a file." They tracked, hot and thirsty. They began to sweat through their clothes. They began to smell of sweat. They could not stop to urinate. If they did stop, the others would go on leaving them alone in this foreign tangle of wildness. The boots and straps made blisters. The blisters bled.

Suddenly the leader stopped. He told them to sit down on the ground in a circle. Then their leader told them what they were to do next. He said, "You are to chose one man to shoot at, one man who will go ahead, deep into the jungle. After one half hour, the rest of you will hunt him down and kill him."

Simon felt his brain go numb. He saw pictures of home in his mind's eye. He thought of the lovely girl in the garden. He felt nothing. He said nothing. He wanted to die. No one moved. All of the young men sat in silence. Some moaned, but their leader repeatedly told them to be silent.

The minutes reached to an eternity. Simon had no idea how long they sat there. It felt like days, or years, or light years. He heard the other young men cry out in protest. He heard the leader yell, "Shut-up!" He barely heard the leader repeat the order to choose one man as a target. Then silence.

It felt to Simon as if a thousand thick nightmares came all at once. Simon had to move through the thickness and he could not. As if he were not himself, as if he were a second person from inside himself, he rose to his feet. He heard, as if from a long way off, his own voice speaking clearly, offering to be the target. "I will be the target. I will go ahead into the jungle."

As Simon opened his eyes he saw that all of the young men were doing the same thing he had done. Each man was offering to be the one who would be hunted down and killed. Each man was willing to die for the others.

The leader watched and waited until they were all on their feet. Their voices called and mingled in the dark trees. They heard each man say that he would be the one, the one to be hunted down and killed. Tears streamed down the leader's face. He collapsed to the floor weeping and laughing at the same time. He lay on the ground shaking. When he finally rose to his feet he screamed a wild cry, the cry of a lion or elephant in painful anguish. Then he was silent.

They all sat on the jungle floor. No one spoke until dark fell and the chill of the earth crept out of the ground. Slowly their leader rose and told them to get up. He lit a powerful cellight and led them on through the jungle along a path that widened as they progressed so that gradually they could walk beside each other.

The leader walked, head down, quietly. At the edge of the jungle he stopped, turned, and told his companions, "If you had not all volunteered to be the one to die, we would have had to kill the chosen man." They looked at one another. They walked on in silence.

That night as Simon bathed he wondered if he would ever experience this kind of fatigue again, wondered if he could survive it twice. He ate whatever food was put before him, went into the toilets, vomited, fell into his bed, prayed his Fourth Prayer: an earnest prayer of thanksgiving.

Then he slept.

Chapter 7
THE FIFTH PRAYER

"Earth will provide if we encourage her,
help her, and cooperate with her."
Fernleaf of the Americas LW490
NEW BOTANY TEXT III

"The earth is a garden, the garden of my Lord, and
He walks in his garden in the cool of the day."
American Folk Hymn

Again, morning began with bells. Servers brought food. One young man asked Simon, "Are you enjoying your visit to the Holy Structure?" He behaved as if he knew nothing of the jungle, the shooting, of the possibility that some of the young men might be dead, killed by their companions. Simon felt as if he lived in two worlds. In one he was cared for tenderly. In the other world he faced hideous realities he never could have imagined before coming to this place.

The meal completed, Servers led the way past the food tables past the kitchens, outside to a garden, a garden much like the one behind his house at home in the Colony. A garden with vegetables, fruit trees, grapevines, herbs, roots. But this garden lay before him, spread in all directions, beyond his line of sight. Water sprinklers attached to the glass ceiling sprayed the growing produce. Drip lines shaped a grid, watering the trees. If Simon squinted his eyes, he imagined he could see grains growing in fields in the distance. He was not sure.

The garden looked good, wholesome and clean, too good to be true after the experiences of the last two days. He wondered if another Priest or Priestess would tell him the food was poisoned, or say the men could not eat this food. He wondered if they had hidden some ugly truth from his sight.

A Priestess called them together. When the men were gathered, she said, "I want to explain to you about this garden." This handsome woman was about the same age as Simon's mother. Her hands looked worn, the grain of her fingers dark with soil, her nails short. Over her robes she wore an apron with many pockets; each pocket held a gardening tool. She wore a deep brimmed hat to shade her smiling face.

The men started to ask questions about the food production, food storage, food preparation. She ignored them all. One of the men from his group in the jungle asked if he might eat some of the fruit on the trees. Again she ignored the question. She simply said, "You may spend the day working in the garden. Tools and hats are in the sheds behind you. Be nice to the plants. Remember always - they feed you. The clay jars hold cool water if you are thirsty." She ignored all of their questions and walked away.

No tricks? No horrors? No one asked to kill a companion? Simon didn't trust the Priestess or the garden. He watched the other young men. They were watching, too. After a while he saw one of his companions lean over, pluck a cherry tomato, hold it up for all to see, put it up to his mouth, chew, and swallow it. Silence. They waited quietly for him to grab his gut in pain, to die right there in front of them. He did neither. He seemed just fine. He smiled.

The idea of working in this garden sounded safe. Simon could hardly wait. He walked slowly to the tool shed, put on a hat, gathered up an armload of tools, and then realized he didn't know what needed to be done. Carefully he put the tools back and pulled the string up tight under his chin so the hat would not fall off. He walked back out into the vegetable garden.

He looked at the plants. They appeared to be healthy, vigorous, needing nothing. He walked over to a fruit tree, felt the bark, and picked a fruit, a peach. He used the sleeve of his robe to rub off the peach fuzz, and ate the smooth pink fruit. It took a few minutes to realize he was alive. Relieved, Simon wanted to work. He wanted to do anything, anything, which would help make the earth a better place to live. A garden seemed a good place to start. He went back to the shed for a hoe.

He had to search for a weed but when he found one, using the corner of the hoe-blade he lifted the weed tidily from the earth, hand carried it to what he was sure was a compost pit. Other young men arrived with weeds. One man found a handful of overripe fruit and tossed it on the pile. Chickens wandered in and amongst the plantings, pecking at bugs, eating larva. Off to one side of the herb garden, a pen kept goats from foraging in the plants. Some of the young men were trying to guess which foods from the garden the goats would eat. They offered greens and carrots. The goats nibbled at the vegetables, eating from the young men's bare hands.

The men spoke to each other, not wearing their translators, but no on seemed to care. They jabbered, sang songs from their homelands, laughed at the patient labor involved in finding enough work to keep them busy. They could not find enough hard work to make them tired, but there was profound rest in this wholesome work, rest needed badly after the trials of the last two days.

The words the Priestess had spoken, the words about how the garden feeds the people, rang through Simon's head. Her words reminded him of an old-song, a folk-song he had heard his grandmother sing. Her song had been about the earth, the earth as a garden of the Lord. Grandmother's song admonished the people to be gentle with the earth, as it was the source of their life's food, as the sun was the source of their life's heat.

He tried to remember the tune but singing was not a talent he had practiced. He vowed he would sing more when he did his work at home, that he would make a point of learning the old songs his grandmother sang. It had not seemed noteworthy at home, but Simon now remembered his father humming a tune when he worked at his Craft. His mother always sang snatches of songs when she worked in the garden. So did his sisters.

The young men hoed, trimmed, dug, visited and sang as they worked in the garden. Food appeared on huge platters at some point during the day, most of it was still on the plates when the work was done. They had eaten what they wanted from the ample garden while they wandered through searching for jobs, searching for the trimming, hoeing, digging, cleaning, all the chores a garden requires. It was nightfall when they finally stopped their work, put away their garden tools, and removed their wide brimmed hats.

That night they splashed and bathed in warm outdoor pools, which caught the drips from the slanted glass roof. They dressed in the clean, robes they found spread on bushes. Draping his towel to dry on the same bushes, Simon took a deep breath of the fragrance of earth, tree, flower, compost, vegetable, and

71

grains. Food, he thought, precious food. He spoke aloud to himself, "Never take food for granted again."

The Priestess led them to cots set up under the heavy branches of green willow trees. They slipped between clean linens and slept. Simon dreamed of fruits splitting wide, of the seeds rotting on the ground.

Simon did not pray before sleep. The young men had prayed together in the garden. It had not been planned. It just happened. After the first man had tried the tomato, found it safe to eat, the others had gone from plant to plant sampling the fruits of the garden. As they became thirsty, they gathered around the water jars taking turns drinking the cool water. In groups of three or four they found themselves spontaneously saying the prayer spoken the world over, "Grant us Oh Goddess and God of Earth and All-Being, food for our bodies and love for our souls. Be it so for all the people." Simon figured he must have prayed his Fifth Prayer a dozen times or more this day. The work done in this fruitful garden felt like prayer, prayer without the need for language.

Chapter 8
SIXTH PRAYER

"It remains to be seen if it is really safe, as the Ancients believed, for knowledge to be the province of all."

Guinna of the Artic LW590
RIGHTS OF THE PEOPLE
CONFERENCE: WHITE PAPER

WAKE UP! WAKE UP! NOW!" Simon, lost deep in his dreams, lost in heavy restful sleep, felt the tug of wakefulness. Several young Servers ran through the garden admonishing the men for sleeping when there was work to be done. The Servers laughed, nudging the sleepy young men in their beds, distributing fresh towels, then disappearing through glass doors Simon did not recall from the night before. From what he could see, the glass doors opened onto what appeared to be another garden. Vaguely, through the glass, stood the outline of a tall, curved building.

Simon awoke suddenly to the realization that there were only two days, two prayers, two circles left to enter. He found it difficult to remember what he had been like before he had come to this place, before he experienced what he had seen and done here. He had heard his parents speak of rebirth, and he had dismissed the idea as some old religious notion, something that may have happened to other people, but not to him. Rebirth was nothing Simon had considered as a relevant experience in his life. And yet he felt as though he had entered the Holy Structure as a boy, and now he felt he had lived several lives in as many days.

Simon felt much older, much more frightened than he had been five days ago. This fear was not the boyish fear of wondering about new places. This was a fear deep in the core of his being, deep in a part of himself he did not recall bringing along with him from home. He had grown a new place for the storage of this fear - and this knowledge.

Simon and his companions dressed in the robes which had been laid out for them in the night, robes of soft many-colored linen, a colored tie for the waist, leather sandals for their feet. Once through the glass doors, out on the patios, food was brought to tables clustered under deep blue wisteria. There were trays of fresh melon, sticky rice with slices of mango, deep bowls of muffins made from many grains and nuts, jars of honey, cold boiled eggs, chutneys, a sliced vegetable platter, goat cheeses, all the sweet products of the carefully tended food garden.

Simon wondered if the other young men felt as he did about what they had seen in the last few days. He wondered if they all had learned as much, been as afraid, as strangely aware as he had been. He didn't want to speak of these things, afraid the others would laugh, afraid they had known all along the lessons Simon was learning so rapidly and with such power and such intensity. He didn't want to be the only one who was trying to take in more than he could assimilate. He ate slowly, savoring every taste, remembering the gardens where this food was grown, and remembering the peace and restfulness that came of working in that garden.

The food trays were carried away. The men rested on the quiet patios in the shade of the lovely curving vine arbor. The high wall of the building they could see as they looked toward the center of the Holy Structure formed a massive curve, circle shaped, just like each of the other rings they had passed through. This one, however, had the look of buildings at home, like the libraries Simon had seen in some of the Colonies.

This building was constructed of bricks and wooden beams. Heavy vines, which grew over the walls, were carefully trimmed at the windows and doors. Simon had never seen a building constructed of real bricks, or wood beams for that matter. Real bricks had to be made of natural materials, made by hand one at a time.

The Colony buildings Simon recognized, might imitate the natural materials they used for building here at the Holy Structure, but at home they were all built of bioboards and ecomaterials. He knew that the natural materials were too costly, too rare to be used anywhere but here. The clay, the wood, the glass, and the craftsmanship used in every ring of this gargantuan structure were essential to maintaining this place, this place called simply, in every language - The Holy Structure.

They sat in the shade. No one came to tell them what to do next. As they grew weary of sitting, one by one the young men strolled over the long paths that wound through the grass, past flower boarders, to the building. Women carrying books and papers came and went through its huge wooden doors. Simon had seen the women of his Colony going in and out of the Library at home. Men were not allowed to enter. Men had no reason to enter. There was nothing there they needed. Here, at the door of this Library, the young men were not stopped as they were at home. No sign told them to turn back. Actually, it never really occurred to the men at home to go into the Library. It was simply understood that the books, except for the Training Manuals, were for the women.

Simon sat on the stone bench near the entry to the Library until he grew weary of sitting. He stood, stretched, and walked slowly along the path toward the entrance. He couldn't bring himself to go in, so he stood for a while outside of the Library pretending to examine the flowers. He began to feel silly, so he walked into the building. As his eyes grew accustomed to the dark of the paneled wood, the oil lamps and candles, he could see a great cavernous room filled with shelves.

The walls and the alleys of shelves were lined from floor to ceiling in all directions with books. There were books in stacks, books of every color. There were bookbindings of cloth, of leather, of wood, of paper. Tall books, skinny books, fat books, stumpy books, books of every size a book could be, crammed the shelves. There were scrolls of linen and papyrus. Stones had been carved with curious forms. Small round disks in tall boxes you could see through, large flat disks in paper wrappers, coils of tape, conical shapes filled the glass fronted cases.

The only books Simon had ever been given to read were the early Training Manuals, the social texts that presented the rules for people living together in families and in larger societal groups. He had dutifully studied the manuals in his Training, studied the skills and information for the work he might be asked to do. Most of what Simon had read was presented on a telescreen in the form of study questions with quiz choices. He had held very few actual books in his lifetime. Now, he wanted to remove just one from the shelves, hold it in his hand to see what it felt like. He did not know if another violent truth lurked in its pages. He wanted to hold and read one book, to see what it said. He did not even care what subject it covered, or what it said.

Simon looked around. No signs forbade taking a book off a shelf. He still didn't trust what might happen. The new fears came again. So many horrible sights and events had come into his young life in the place called The Holy Structure. He looked around again, took a breath, and reached for a dark red book, a book with gold edges on the pages, a book with paper so thin he could almost see the print on the back of the page.

His fears forgotten, he turned the volume over in his hands. He felt the edges, ran his thumbnail along the groove next to the backing. Simon let the book fall open to a page where it divided by habit. Someone had written in the margins, made notes about their thoughts on the subject at hand. He could not imagine writing in one of the Manuals. This book reminded him of the book encased in plastine at the Colony Museum where his father had taken him to see examples of the Craft of Woodworking. While there, he saw a plain black book inscribed with gold writing: *HOLY BIBLE.* He remembered being curious, but not as interested as he was in the construction of the case which held it.

He turned his attention to the deep red book in his hands. He thumbed slowly through the pages, stopped, then read the words: "Or I was attracted by the passage of wild pigeons from this wood to that, with a slight quivering winnowing sound and carrier haste...", then "...and outlandish spotted salamander, a trace of Egypt and the Nile, yet our..." Simon read on through scattered sections from the pages. He could not understand the meaning even though he could read the words.

A woman stepped up to him and asked, "Are you finding what you are looking for?"

Simon stammered, "Well, I don't know for sure, but I…"

He tried to admit to himself that he did not know what he was looking for. He stood silent, waiting, hoping she would speak again.

The woman said, "I am a Librarian. It is my job to help people in the Library. You might find something interesting in the children's books, something that would help you to begin to understand the use of books." She pointed to an aisle on the other side of a long hall.

Simon felt a little foolish. He wanted to start with the book he found first, but he could not. He nodded at the woman and she started to walk away.

She turned back to Simon and motioned for him to follow her. She led the way to the adjacent section of the library where the chairs and tables were small, child-sized. Boys and girls sat in some of the chairs, reading from the books they held on their laps. The Librarian sat down at one of the taller tables and began to copy from the large brown book she carried. Reluctantly, Simon went over to the children's books, searched until he found one written in American. This book had drawings of delightful animals talking with each other and talking with humans. Simon read a bit. He stood amazed. He knew the story. His mother had told it to him and his sisters over and over; so had his grandmother. They had told it just as it was written, but without the book.

The pictures that seemed real to Simon were a lot like the ones he had made up in his head as his mother told the story. It had never occurred to Simon that a story might come with its own pictures. He liked the pictures in his head, his own private pictures to go with each story.

He scrunched down into one of the little chairs. He hardly noticed several other young men, their long legs folded cricket style, or sitting on the floor with a book in their lap. Simon turned page after page in disbelief. He picked up another book, a story he knew, a story his mother had told him over and over, a story whose truth and imagined pictures were part of his life. He read for a while then he simply sat, staring into space.

He thought to himself: Books tell stories. Books have pictures.

Simon sat for a long time. He got up, walked back toward the entrance and returned to the book he had first selected. He turned to the beginning of the book and read: "*WALDEN. I. ECONOMY.* When I wrote the following pages, or rather the bulk of them, I lived alone, in the woods, a mile from any neighbor, on the shore of Walden Pond, in Concord, Massachusetts, and earned my living by the labor of my two hands only." Simon read on.

Simon knew he could understand the words this man named Thoreau had written in this book. He looked around at all of the books he would never be allowed to read. He felt anger rise in his throat. Two questions burned in his brain: Why did the women have the privilege of using the library? Why not the men? The answer must be in the books, somewhere.

The woman who had directed him to the children's books was still studying at a nearby table. She had seemed friendly enough when she had spoken to Simon before. He decided to ask her his question. As he walked up to the library table where she studied, she put her glasses down on the table and turned her attention to Simon. Simon felt shy about asking but his anger was winning out over his reluctance. The right of women to books had been the accepted norm for so long that his need to question the reason felt strange, unreal. He felt as though he had no right to ask his question.

The woman listened attentively as Simon explained about the book with the childhood story in it, about the pictures, and about the red and gold book by a man named Thoreau. She did not interrupt. She seemed quiet and calm as he asked about the tradition of books being the right and privilege of women, about the Manuals he studied in school, about his desire to learn from all of these varied books.

She waited patiently for Simon to relate his experience and to finish his questions about the books. When he was done, she said, "Many young men have the same experience, and the same questions. It will all be explained following the evening meal." She put her glasses on and returned to her studies. He walked away, afraid to ask her any more questions.

Simon spent the remainder of the day selecting a book, reading a few pages, then selecting another, finding a new subject in the vast halls and repeating the process. He read a little about history, about philosophy, mathematics, design, architecture, art, agriculture. He read scientific treatises on physics, astronomy, medicine, nuclear energy, biophysics, and physiology. He read a few paragraphs on as many subjects as he could find. Many he did not understand. He read bits of poetry, a few lines from a short story, and lines from long fictional books he knew he would never be allowed to complete.

He read from the books in a room dedicated to a man named William Shakespeare. Much of what he read he understood to be obsolete, or too advanced for his level of education. He began to feel unintelligent, even stupid. Simon had always felt good about himself. His parents had told him how smart he was. Had they lied?

Somewhere in the distance a chime rang. A Priestess walked by saying, "The library will now close for dinner. It is time to put away the book you are reading." Simon was beginning to understand that the world of knowledge was far more vast than he could ever have imagined, than he could possibly grasp. He had only begun to sense that the subjects covered in those books were all somehow related to each other. It was like trying to think about outer space. He couldn't manage it. His brain just quit. His hunger growled and his hand went to his abdomen. Food. Yes. Food might help.

Their dinner was served in a large hall somewhere in the inner workings of the Holy Structure. A woman in a black robe entered the hall, walked up to a podium, tapped the wood with a gavel, and said, "May I have your attention."

The young men, done with their dinner for a while now, turned their chairs toward her and sat back to listen. They had experienced a remarkable day. They had spoken of it during dinner to one another. This day had ended with more questions than answers for each of the men. Simon wanted to ask his questions, but he was afraid the rage he felt would choke his voice. Perhaps another young man felt the same rage. Perhaps another young man would ask what Simon wanted to know, would ask the troubling questions Simon wanted answered.

The woman began to speak: "The black robe I wear is a symbol, a copy of the ancient robes worn by scholars who studied the books in the olden days before the Last War." She went on to explain, "For most of human history scholarship was the province of men. Only in the last few hundred years before the

Last War were women allowed to read or to study. Learning, for the most part, was historically set aside for men. In some countries the women where never allowed to read."

"Men directed the choice of subjects in the student institutions called Colleges and Universities. They had the power over who could learn what subject, who could train for what kind of work. They even had control of which books would be studied and by whom. Further, they wrote most of the books, which were studied, and determined the way the knowledge in those books would be used. "

She did not pause to allow questions, but went on with the explanation, "The men determined which subjects were studied first, which second, and third, and so on. The formal study of philosophy and religion come quite early, along with astronomy and mathematics." She went on with her lecture and explanations. Simon began to listen to his own inner voice instead of hers. He knew he was missing what she said, but he couldn't get over how much there was to know that he would never be able to know, even if it was allowed. He was filled with a deep sense of sadness.

He began to feel anger at the woman, and at the society, which kept him from this knowledge. He began to wonder how the women managed to get such power? How did they take over the knowledge of the world to keep it as their special province? Who gave them this right?

Simon couldn't remember ever having been so angry. The clarity of his anger snapped him out of his day-dream. He wakened to hear the woman say, " …and so the women took over the libraries and the laboratories because for most of history, men had used knowledge for power through war and control of the financial institutions and commerce. They didn't know how to stop. They didn't know how to live in peace and care for each other."

Simon knew he had missed something important, the answer to his question. Looking around at the other young men, he saw that they seemed as agitated as he. The woman said, "Here at the Holy Structure, when a woman completes her studies, she can select her own name. She is then called by that name for the rest of her life. Further, she has the obligation to live up to the meaning of that name. I chose the name Truth. I will answer any questions you might have."

The young men just sat there. Someone would start to ask a question, then stop. One young man stood and asked, "Will the men ever be allowed in the libraries again?"

Truth replied, "The possibility of that was considered at a recent conference but not settled. The fear of war is still very deep in the consciousness of women."

Simon thought about two questions he had prepared when he had applied as a youth/student representative to attend the Rights of the People Conference held two years before. Another boy had been chosen to go. Simon realized that his questions had been answered by the events of the past few days. He had begun to understand what war did to the earth. He had seen what the nuclear devastation did to the people and the planet. He decided he didn't really want to know the answer to his questions.

The questions swirled in his head. Is that what men had done with knowledge? Is that what men had done to earth? He felt sick at heart, not sure he wanted to be a man. There must be some explanation. There had to be. This was too terrible. If men could write these beautiful books, if men could create these perfect gardens, if they could work at a beautiful Craft as his father did, how could they have come to the Last War?

For the first time in his young life, Simon experienced the feeling of shame. He had never had cause to feel shame. This shame was deep in his being, deep in the fact of his manhood. He was ashamed simply because he was alive. He was ashamed because he was a man.

Simon wept. Many of the young men wiped away tears.

Questions began to rise from the room. The young men, lifting their heads from their inner turmoil, wanted to know how it had come to this.

Truth told them the story, simply, directly: "After the Last War, the women who could produce children, did so. The women also studied in the basements of the universities and libraries, since those institutions were seldom the targets of war, and many were still standing. The men did the physical work. Women who could not bear children took positions of responsibility for the community. The women could not allow any possibility of war. Fortunately, there were few weapons left which could function.

"Very gradually, the women became scientists. They became community planners. Perhaps the men were ashamed. No one knows for sure. The records from that time are few and far between, as there was a limited supply of paper and that had to be used for peaceful endeavors. It was all a very long time ago."

Truth's expression was sad, but she went on. She looked out at these young men. She had said these words many times to many men, and she felt she understood what they were experiencing.

"Over time the safe places of the earth were colonized. The natural products were gradually replaced by synthetic ones, in order to save what was left of the natural world. The first major task was the trial and error search for new energy sources. Photolight cells were a significant source. Anyone with a hopeful idea brought it forth and the idea was tested, no matter how absurd it may have seemed. Because the women, afraid for their families, afraid for the children, were open to new ideas, discoveries came quickly. This was not a commercial endeavor; this was a matter of survival."

"Family structure and world population had to be controlled because resources were at a premium. The use of sea water to make plastine was one of the first major scientific breakthroughs. Anything, which was not contaminated, was used."

Simon felt dizzy. He shook his head. He found the courage to stand and ask, "How long ago was this? How long did it take to build the first Colony? How did they do the work that was needed?" The questions spun in his head.

Truth smiled around the room at the young men so eager with their questions. She looked at Simon and said, "I cannot possibly answer all of your questions, but I will try in the time left this evening." She knew their thinking would be bombarded with questions for months. Their questions, which never would be answered, didn't really matter. She had no way to explain this to these frightened young men,

Truth closed, saying, "And so, it took more than a thousand years to create a world in which there is no more war, no disease, no poverty, and no bigotry. It took five hundred years to build the Holy Structure here in the middle of the Unending Desert. The building goes on, the learning goes on. Peace goes on! We ask one more thing of you. We ask you not speak of your experiences here at the Holy Structure, not to each other, not to anyone at home."

Truth walked out of the hall. They could ask no more questions. They sat in silence, not speaking even to one another. Simon slowly realized that he knew many men who had been on their Pilgrimage, and he had not heard any of them speak of it.

This was the eve of their final day, the night before they were to enter the last ring. Simon wondered if there would be a ceremony or a feast. He had reached the place in himself where nothing would have surprised him. By now though, the idea of some kind of formal occasion seemed unnecessary, almost absurd.

The young men began asking each other all the questions Truth had not answered. How did the women know what to study? Did some of the men want to study as they had before? What happened to all the old weapons of war? Are any of them still hidden somewhere? Did the men become angry with the women?

They sat in the great hall waiting for something, anything, to happen. Nothing happened. The doors behind them, the doors that led back to the gardens, were closed with great bars laid across them to serve as locks. They could only go inward, through doors closer to the center of the Holy Structure. Moving toward the last ring, they passed along gravel paths. It was late in the evening and the gently curving paths were lit by torchlight.

Simon found the walk to be restful. The questions, which

had burned in his brain, were fading. They came to a circle of doors opening on to bathing rooms with fresh towels and clean robes. Here they showered, and looked around for the beds which were usually waiting for them. There were no beds, no mats on the floor, only a series of small doors opening inward.

For the first time since they entered the Holy Structure, they did not sleep together. A Priest came through one of the doors and said simply, "Will each man please come now and select a door. Each of you will sleep in a room alone."

By this time the men had learned to follow instructions without asking more questions. Simon wanted to sit and talk with the other young men, but he could not. He entered his cell, slipped into his bed, and prayed his sixth prayer, a quiet prayer for rest, peace of mind, and the strength to accept the unknowable.

Chapter 9
THE SEVENTH PRAYER

"We must defend our rights as persons through the extended development of a stable social organization."

Olain of the North LW78
FIRST WOMEN'S CONFERENCE

"ON THE SEVENTH DAY THEY RESTED"

Those were the words carved over the doorway of every public building in the Colony. Simon had seen them so often he never questioned their meaning. Like traffic direction signs, they were understood as soon as one could read. If not understood, taken for granted, their meaning taken for common knowledge.

Simon awoke in his little cell to the sound of children's voices. He looked around at the simple furnishings, the cot, one chair, a towel rack holding clean towels, a clay bowl of flowers on a small wooden table. A Priest's robe and sash hung on a peg by the door. Over the door hung a dark wooden plaque carved with the words, "ON THE SEVENTH DAY THEY RESTED."

Simon dressed quickly and walked into the hallway. He knew beyond this next wall he would enter the last circle. The inner doors stood open. He could see children, children playing. He could hear them laughing. He stepped through the door onto a smooth brick floor. Beyond the bricks, grass, and beyond the grass, he saw a circular pool. Trees, some with rope and board swings attached, shaded the grass. Some of the swings carried children swinging back and forth in the dappled shade. Little children, under school age, played ball, looked at books, ran in a game of tag, listened to stories read to them by Elders. Simon couldn't help but wonder what it would be like to grow up being read to from all those amazing books he had seen in the library. He set aside the thought, as it would do no good to wonder. He knew he would never know.

Couples walked hand in hand on the lawn. Some of them fed the geese and ducks, which swam on the broad moat surrounding the center pavilion. At what appeared to be the exact center, there stood a tall, needle shaped spire. Pergolas shaded by wisteria and passion vines sheltered people eating picnics from brown cloth bags. A few Elders sat at tables playing some kind of game with flat cards and little square disks. It all made for a peaceful sight. Flowers grew in beds and boxes, arranged so the eye discovered color at every turn.

Occasionally, here and there over the grass, stood a slab of marble, perhaps rosy or gray, perhaps pale green or black. Fine lines of names carved into the stone, created horizontal patterns on the shiny surfaces. No statuary, no ornamental art, nothing artificial blotted this quiet backyard kind of space. Simon thought of home, of his own back yard, of the park in the center of his Colony. He felt tears behind his eyes. Simon wanted to go home. He wanted to see his cousin, his mother and father, his sisters. He wanted to get back to his everyday life with the people he loved so much. He had forgotten to miss them. He had been so totally absorbed in the life of this place. He was filled with guilt at the idea that he could have forgotten them at all.

Simon sat at one of the shaded tables. No Servers came, no instructions arrived from a Priestess or Priest. No ceremony here, simply the peace and quiet of people enjoying the day. The thought of home was more than he could hold. Tears filled his eyes and ran down his cheeks. He did not care if the others saw him cry.

A young male Server slid into the chair across the table from Simon. Simon wiped his eyes on the sleeve of his robe. The Server smiled at Simon, got up and went over to an open window in a small stone building, picked up a tray and returned with tea, fruit, goat cheese and warm breads. Simon hadn't realized how hungry he was. The Server offered food to Simon. They sat at a table and ate together. Simon did not speak. He did not know what he would say and he was a little afraid of what the Server might say.

Filled with a longing for home, feeling incomplete, Simon just looked at the Server eating so peacefully, watching the children play in this happy, quiet place. He wanted to ask so many questions. Where was the imagined final ceremony? When the sexual ritual? Was there some proclamation of manhood? Were the other young men as troubled as Simon? The agony of the unanswered questions, frustration at his inability to ask, his longing for home, prevented Simon from enjoying the lovely garden. The Server seemed sympathetic, but said nothing.

Simon looked around at the scene before him. Curiosity got the better of him and he asked the Server, "Whose children are these?" The Server smiled and said, "Ours. Well, everyone's actually. We live in community."

Simon did not see any traditional family groups, no mother-father-children-grandparents. He looked more closely. The children were of every racial group imaginable. So were the elders. So were the couples. Who are these people? How did they get here? For an instant Simon thought he saw the lovely young woman who led him to lovemaking with the whole of his body and soul. Could she be pregnant with a child of his? Could the beautiful children of this garden be the offspring of the Pilgrims? How would he ever know? He turned to ask the Server, but the young man was gone.

Simon felt abandoned, abandoned and betrayed. For the first time in his young life, Simon felt what it was like not to be cared for immediately, to turn to people with questions and find they had gone.

He had no idea how long he sat there in the garden. His brain numbed, and a peevish anger grew slowly. Occasionally someone would sit down with him, bring him a drink or food, sit for a while, and then leave.

Gradually his questions faded. Gradually he realized that his home and his family, his cousin, his sisters, his Colony with its work and friends was all that he really wanted. Here there were too many questions, too many unanswerable questions. Simon stretched out on the grass under a willow tree and drifted into a fitful sleep. He was tired deep down inside where sleep might help and where it might not. He slept a dreamless sleep.

When Simon awoke, twilight was on the garden. The children and Elders were gone. The young man who brought him his breakfast was sitting at a nearby table reading a book. Another question about books and why men can't read them jumped into Simon's mind, but he set it aside. He had only one question now and he didn't know whom to ask. Simon stretched and flexed his sleepy body, then stood, walked over to the young man and asked, "How do I get home?"

The Server laughed, handed Simon a sandwich, bade him sit for a bit, then answered, "Tomorrow morning you will go home by the usual route." Simon was astonished that the Server spoke his language. He must have looked surprised because the Server smiled and then laughed a little. The young man extended his hand and said, "My name is Nathan. What's yours?"

Simon blurted out, "Simon. I didn't know you could talk to me." He wanted to ask more questions, but he didn't.

He smiled at the Server named Nathan and stared into the evening, into the garden in the fading light, wondering what time it was back home. Home! Home! He sighed a deep sigh and let his shoulders fall, let his whole being relax for the first time since he arrived in this place. A sweet release.

After he finished eating, the Server began to talk with Simon. He asked Simon if he needed anything. Simon couldn't think what he might need other than the life he knew in the Colony. The Server said to Simon, "Do you have any questions?"

Simon looked around at his surroundings and asked, "Please tell me about this garden."

The young man said, "This garden forms the cemetery for the Holy Structure. Some people ask to be cremated, their ashes spread on the Unending Desert, but some want to be buried. Their bodies are placed in a vertical hole during the night, the grass replaced, and the person's name carved on one of the marble walls. The garden never changes, no mounds, no ceremony, just this quiet, evergreen flowering garden."

On into the evening Simon asked his questions. Nathan answered. He told Simon, "It took more than five hundred years to build the Holy Structure. Each of the Ancient Crafts has been relearned, restored, and practiced in order to build the structure, in order to preserve the Craft. Nails are forged by hand, beams are cut from whole trees, tiles are formed over the thighs of the workers, then, the wet clay tile is dried in the sun. Glass is rolled and cut by hand, colored glass is made into windows, then sectioned together with strips of a soft metal called lead."

Simon asked, "Where do you get the natural raw materials?"

"From all over the world, wherever they are left", said Nathan.

Simon asked, "Tell me about the water. Where does it come from here in the Unending Desert?"

The Server said, "Rainwater from the heavy rain season is gathered, stored, and carried by means of an elaborate aqueduct through clay pipes. The pipes were formed and fired in ovens, which had been constructed of hand made bricks. Pots and bowls were thrown on the potter's wheel, silverware forged and hammered from several metals including silver, beads blown from glass, wood carved for ornament and decoration, cloth woven on shuttle looms, sandals formed on the last. All of the Ancient Crafts are kept alive and active in the Holy Structure. In case they are ever be needed."

Simon asked if he would be allowed to see the Ancient Crafts at work. He had seen nothing of the working Crafts except for the results of the work as he had passed through the rings to this, the center. His mind was full to overflowing; he could not possibly digest all he had learned. It would take a lifetime to really understand. Even then, Simon was not sure he would ever fully understand the differences between a world where everything is crafted by hand and the world of his Colony where the natural resource is protected by law, where almost everything he and his family used was synthetic and manufactured by machinery.

The one question he was afraid to ask kept going through his head, "What did the Server mean when he said, 'In case they are ever needed.' "

Simon began to understand the value of the few relics each family treasured so. Nathan said, "You will be able to pass through the Craft Halls your way out of the Holy Structure. You will not be able to stay long enough to learn a Craft. The Elders of your Colony are the ones to decide if you will be chosen to learn a Craft. If you are chosen, either your father, or another Colony Craftsman will need to teach you. Simon, was your father chosen to learn a Craft?"

Simon said, "Yes. He works with wood."

"You are blessed." said the Server. Simon was puzzled about being "blessed".

It was late, dark, and a chill settled on the garden. Simon watched as some of the other young men and women were walking out to the moat, walking quickly along the paths to warm up. Nathan offered Simon a woolen robe against the cold, and it felt good to gather the robe around his shoulders. They walked out to the water's edge. Simon had forgotten all about the needle shaped spire in the center. As they approached the moat, he saw it was much farther away than he would have guessed. The garden was so perfectly proportioned that distance was inestimable. The moat was deep, and at least two miles in diameter.

The needle in the center was tall, slender, a silver color. It seemed to sit on a small cement pad with an elaborate iron fence surrounding it. Simon had almost forgotten to ask about the spire. So many questions had buzzed through his head, some answered, but so many remained unanswered. This lofty needle seemed an anticlimax. When he finally asked about the needle, he was almost too sleepy to listen an answer. It didn't matter. All Simon could think of was going home.

The Server did not answer Simon's question. He stood at an outer railing looking at the needle. Many other Servers stood near the moat or on the grass, looking at the needle. Simon saw that most of the young men he remembered meeting were here in the garden. Again he thought he caught a glimpse of the lovely young woman from the wild garden. He thought he saw her walking with another young man. It couldn't matter now. It could not matter, as he knew he would never see her again. Tomorrow Simon would go home, home to his Cristin whom he loved, home to the world he knew, the world that made sense to him.

The woman named Green Grass walked across the lawn. The woman named Truth walked with her. Between them was another woman, older, and a bit taller, her long gray hair twined into a single braid that fell almost to her knees. She wore a woven multicolored robe, glass beads, silver earrings, and the plain leather sandals worn by everyone here at the Holy Structure.

She paused at the water's edge, then said in a clear voice, "Please turn on your translators. I want to talk with all of the young men who are Pilgrims before you begin your journey through the Craft Halls. When you have passed through the Craft Halls, you shall go on to your homes." She went on to say, "I am quite sure you all have asked someone about this slender needle in the center of the Holy Structure."

Simon was tired to the point of exhaustion, but he desperately wanted to know this last answer to this last question. The woman began by saying, "My name is Peace. The needle in the center of the Holy Structure is a type of rocket, one of many placed all around the world, deep in silos hidden in every Colony on earth." She paused then went on to explain, "The women of the earth became sick and exhausted with the wars men had created, so we have taken the power unto ourselves. "

"After men devised the nuclear bomb, they went on to construct a neutron bomb. This new bomb was in the test stage when the Last War started as the result of a dispute over clean water and a substance called 'oil'. The neutron bomb, if detonated, would have destroyed all life, leaving man-made structures empty and foolish in the deadly winds left in its trail."

"After the Last War, the women could no longer tolerate the sight of their dead children, no longer tolerate the idea of their sons and daughters fighting meaningless, unwinable wars. They became angry at war, and angry with the men who made war against each other. Some of the old women realized they had been partially responsible for the destruction, as they had allowed the men to make these unholy wars on each other.

"The women concluded that bombs which devastated society and destroyed people did not frighten most of the men, but they terrified the women. The old women who survived the Last War remembered all too well how the governments had referred to weapons of destruction as 'peace-keepers'. After the

Last War the women concluded that if a tool, a bomb, could keep the peace, it must not destroy life. It must change the way people live. A bomb, a so-called peacekeeper, would have to eliminate luxury. It would have to make life harder without killing anyone. It must make the idea of 'winning' into an absurd concept."

The young Pilgrims stood silent, listening. Simon was suddenly alert where as a few minutes ago he had been sleepy and inattentive.

Peace went on to say, "The needle rockets contain a kind of explosive device which, if detonated, would not hurt the natural aspects of the earth, nor would it kill or maim people or animals. It would simply destroy everything synthetic, everything not-natural."

She continued, "I hope you have enjoyed your stay, and I hope you have learned much from your Pilgrimage to the Holy Structure.". She thanked them for coming, and told them to return through the open doors to the beds they had last slept in. In the morning they would be instructed on their return trip. Peace, Green Grass, and Truth then strolled around the lawn saying good evening and thanking the men for coming, wishing them a good trip home, shaking hands or hugging the young men. They refused to answer any more questions.

These women looked and sounded just like the women Simon knew at home. Green Grass could have been his aunt, as they looked so much alike. The reality of what Peace had said did not have any real meaning to Simon; it did not soak in to his consciousness, until he sat on the edge of his cot removing his sandals.

Silly thoughts skipped through his mind. Could he keep

his sandals? Would he have to walk that long mile out as he had coming in? The implications of the needle rocket were more than Simon could take in all at once. But he saw clearly that if those rockets were ever launched, his life, everyone's life, in all Colonies, everywhere, would be very different. If war came would his father become a more important man in the Colony because he kept a Craft? What did it really mean to be important? The concept of important became confusing. Absurd thoughts clattered off the walls of his brain. Contradiction after contradiction rose and fell, his thoughts more jumbled than ever.

At home in the Colony only a few people were chosen to work a Craft. Simon knew only his father who worked with wood, and one friend's father who was allowed to cast metal in a small forge in his backyard workshop. If the rockets were detonated, who would ever put the Colony back together so that people could have the goods they needed. How would their clothes be woven? There would be no more biosuits. His grandmother's loom was so slow. Simon wondered if his cousin had ever kissed another man and never told him. Odd, disconnected thoughts ran through his mind.

Simon began to sweat. The more clearly he understood the impact of the needle rockets, the more he soaked his robe. He needed sleep. He needed rest. He went to the baths, slipped into the warm water, praying all the while that the needle rockets would never, never be fired.

Chapter 10
HOME

"Truth has no special time of its own. Its hour is now-always, and indeed then most truly when it seems most unsuitable to actual circumstances."

Albert Schweitzer 1875-1955 CE
THE STRUGGLE FOR TRUTH

It was late in the morning when Simon wakened. He had slept a troubled sleep. He dreamed strange dreams in which he tried to build a doll's house of wood, with no help, no trees to fell, and no nails. He dreamed of his cousin. In his dream he made love with her; he felt sticky against the smooth linens. He wanted to go home.

He wanted to explain these new experiences and feelings to someone but was not at all sure anyone could ever understand how he felt. He knew he couldn't be the only one who had ever felt this way. For the first time since he arrived at this place, he found himself wishing he had his journals, wishing he could write down some of his thoughts. His body jerked involuntarily.

Simon remembered that he had never heard any of the men of his father's age talk about their Pilgrimage. He wondered if any of the older men he knew had written down their thoughts and experiences. Perhaps this was the reason the journals were sealed on a man's eighteenth birthday. He struggled with the strange, disconnected thoughts he was having, and finally, he decided he just didn't care if anyone else understood.

Simon knew one thing. He knew he wanted to go home.

A voice spoke from somewhere saying food would be served in the great hall through the red door. He thought back and tried to remember a red door. It was strange he did not recall a red door either night he had slept there. Perhaps he had simply not been paying attention. This place, this Holy Structure, presented too much that was unexplainable, too much that didn't seem to relate to his life in the Colony. People came and went from unseen places. Voices called giving orders that had to be obeyed. There were too many new ideas, too many new experiences, and they all came at once.

Simon decided it would do no good to try to make sense of the things he had seen. It didn't matter. In fact, so many things didn't matter any more. He followed several other young men who seemed to know where they were going. He passed through the red door into the hall, sat at one of the long tables where Servers brought food, good nourishing food. He ate. Everything tasted good. Wonderful. He relished the taste, the smell, and the feel of the food in his mouth. For some reason he didn't want to forget how good it was simply to sit at a table and eat plain food. He didn't need anything else. His fatigue began to lift.

A tall, gray-haired Priest entered the great hall, asked them to turn on their translators, and then he gave directions to the men for their passage through the Great Craft Halls. They were to form small groups from the tables where they sat.

They were to follow another Priest who would join them soon. That Priest would answer their questions. The men were told they would stay one more night in the Holy Structure. The following day they would return to their homes.

Simon sat at his place until a slender old Priest joined the group at his table. The man bent with age, had gray hair and a twinkle of laughter in his eyes. Simon warmed to the way the old man looked, hoped he would have laughter in his eyes when he grew to that venerable age. His thoughts began to stray. Simon wondered how you manage to have laughing eyes when you are old.

Remembering the needle rockets, he said a quick prayer that he would have the opportunity to become a venerable age. People had died very young when there was war and pestilence, disease and poverty. Simon did not want to die young. He wanted to grow old with his beautiful cousin, whether they were allowed to have children or not. He wanted to do simple, honest work. He wanted to be chosen for a Craft. That, of course, would remain to be seen. He knew he would do what had to be done to live the life he was to live. It was as simple as that.

The group of young men followed the old Priest down the curve of the long hall. They passed through a series of doors, opening onto large workrooms filled with men and women working.

"These are the Great Craft Halls. The first hall, the weaving hall, contains the looms where our fabrics are woven." the old Priest said. The clickity-click of the harnesses, and the swoosh of the shuttles filled the room with a watery sound. The Weavers were intent on their work but able to pause and chat with the young men as they passed by. Weavers called out "hellos" in many languages, as they had no idea what part of the world the groups of men came from. This workroom was airy and light, and the workers seemed cheerful and relaxed.

Simon wanted to ask so many questions. He remembered his great-grandmother at the loom in her small cottage. She must have been in her ninetieth year when Simon watched her weave a food-cloth. Simon walked up to a woman Weaver and asked, "How long did it take you to learn to weave?"

The Weaver smiled and motioned for the old Priest to come answer the question. The Priest said, "She is deaf, but I will answer. The Weavers begin when they are small children on little handlooms. That way they discover whether weaving is the right Craft for them. If not, they try something else. All of the workers in the Great Craft Halls work at that which they love to do." The Priest smiled and led them on.

The men were led away from the Weavers and passed into a smaller room where the workers were bent over benches holding small tools for fine metal work. They worked at grinding stones, and small anvils, while soldering tools rested on coals. Silversmiths made flatware, plates, jewelry, and ornamental bowls. Simon had no idea it would take so long to polish the front piece of one earring for one ear. Here, both men and women wore earrings. Simon marveled at the idea that mankind ever had the time and patience to learn to produce such things by the Crafts? He did not ask his question of the worker this time. This time he asked his question of the Priest. The Priest smiled and said, "People have always had time for beauty if they choose to use their time that way."

The young men spent the day walking from one Craft Hall to the next. Simon was stunned by the wide range of woodworking tools. His father had a few, but these people had tools Simon had never seen, tools from different cultures, held and used in ways he had not seen in his father's shop.

The old Priest explained that the wood-workers shaped wooden objects with tools from all over the Ancient world. When a tool wore out, they had to take time to build a new tool. One entire Craft Hall was devoted to replacing tools without changing their basic, original form and structure, using the original materials if they could be found. "Those Craftsmen are really kept busy. Tools do wear out, and they break from time to time." explained the Priest.

Simon was tired. He was even tired of learning about all the new things he had seen. He wanted to rest, eat, sleep, and start for home. He had seen room after room, Craft after Craft, skills, materials, designs, work done with the hands, work man-and-womankind could not lose, in case, just in case the needle rockets might be set off. One hall held the plans and a miniature model for the aqueducts, which provided the drinking and bathing waters for the Holy Structure. Another model showed waterways, which carried the used water to filtration pools where this precious liquid was made clean again, so it could be used for irrigation. Water! Simon had always taken water for granted. He shook his head at the idea of how childishly innocent, and how foolish he had been before coming to this place.

On this, his last night in the Holy Structure, Simon slept deeply and soundly. He woke in the morning to the sound of music, a lute, a lyre, dulcimer, flute, and tambourine. He smelled the sweet, pungent aroma of fresh food. He went into the bathing pools. Remembering this bath from the first day at the Holy Structure, he sank into the warm water and waited until somebody told him he had to move. He was content. He was bone-weary and more than content to return home. There had been no ceremony of any kind. Was the idea of a ceremony the self-deluding, indulgent imaginings of young school-boys pretending to know what they were in for when they went on their Pilgrimage. Perhaps, Simon thought, it was a story they made up to cope with their fear of the unknown.

It just didn't matter.

Back in the changing rooms, Simon found his family garments carefully folded in a locker bearing his name. He packed them carefully into his travel pack, ashamed he had forgotten these precious relics so easily. He put on his travel suit, his foot coverings. Would someone come and take away the sandals he had worn in the Holy Structure? Could he take them home? He didn't remember seeing sandals in the Colonies. He felt sad. He had come to enjoy the feel of the rough natural fibers against his body, the slip and slide of the sandals on his feet. He had even learned to kick the occasional pebble from between his foot and the leather floor of the sandal.

He wondered what they did with all the robes he had worn. Would the lovely young woman from the garden wash them for another young man? He felt sad at the thought of her sweet face, her beautiful, strong body. He couldn't help but wonder how many other young men she had led into the wonders of lovemaking. At this point a sexual ritual seemed such a silly idea. Simon was embarrassed at his own thoughts. He glanced around, hoping he was not blushing.

The other young men were busy dressing and packing. They did not speak much, knowing they would probably never see each other again. The dark cavern of the first ring of the Holy Structure felt like a familiar place as Simon stepped from the changing rooms into its shadows. The glare of the sun on the sand seen from this direction, seen as a mile toward home, seemed almost inviting.

No one said farewell or goodbye. No Priest or Priestess presented any statement of completion. The Pilgrimage was over. He was walking away from The Holy Structure, a place Simon felt he had known all his life. Simon stepped out onto the sand. The Last Mile had become the last mile once again.

He didn't mind the heat. He held his head up, looking around at the Unending Desert as he walked. He could see clearly the shine and subtle colors of the sand, the pitch and roll of the dunes in the distance. It was beautiful. It was plain. It was peaceful. He thought for a few moments of the young men yet to cross this mile. He brushed away a tear with the back of his hand. He couldn't help but smile.

Simon wondered what he would say to his friends about his Pilgrimage. Probably nothing. Peace had asked them to say nothing. No pledge or promise had been given, but he knew he would not speak of it. He knew deep in some inner place that nothing he might say would be of help to anyone but himself.

Simon kept on walking, going home.

THE BEGINNING